BRING ON THE
MAGIC

D0090404

The Salesman and the Farmer
A DREAMS DIRECT SERIES

By J. Logan Arnold

Printed in the United States of America

ISBN 978-0-615-31415-0

Cover Design by Anthony Sclavi

This book is dedicated to my lovely wife, Runi Jo. Her patient support never wavered in expectancy of success.

TABLE OF CONTENTS

PRELUDE

The Salesman and the Farmer

Within this book the steps are told
That bring your dreams success,
So use them wisely to unfold
The dreams you now possess.

On this very special day, I sit beside my wife in the cockpit of our small sailboat. We are just finishing our second cup of coffee as the sun finally clears the treetops on the highest ridge to the east of us. Anchored in the gin-clear waters of the Caribbean Ocean, our beautiful sailing vessel sits quietly, sheltered from the ever-blowing trade winds by the island of Utilla.

"The winds seem calm for this time of morning," my wife said, already wiping the sweat from her forehead. Usually by now the winter trade winds are blowing a gale.

"Once we sail clear of the island," I said, "I bet that changes. A calm day here and there is the exception, not the rule. But then again, who knows; we just might get lucky."

"It's been a long time in coming, hasn't it?" she said.

"Yes, long indeed; it's hard to believe it's been almost fifteen years now," I replied. It was an ironic twist that brought us here, but we finally made it. We were very fortunate. "We still have a ways to go. Best we get an early start." We both knew that the wind was frequently light earlier in the day.

I made the obligatory captain's inspection around the deck before our departure, checking rigging, sheets and sails. Everything seemed in order.

I first removed the sail ties that secure the mainsail to the boom, and then I connected the sail to the halyard line used to hoist it up the mast. Inside the cabin below deck, my wife went about tidying everything in the galley.

"All secure down here, Sweetie," she yelled up. "Ready when you are."

"I'm ready to bring up the anchor," I told her. "Hoist the mainsail and we'll be on our way."

As the large mainsail reached the top of the mast, my wife took the tiller in hand and I finished pulling the anchor and its chain-rode onto the boat. Our sailboat heeled over slightly as the wind filled her sail and she began to move slowly toward open water, beyond the protection of the island.

"Put her on a course of two hundred seventy degrees," I said, knowing that heading would take us to the far end of Utilla. "Let's see what the winds have in store for us."

We charged across the beautiful blue ocean with my wife at the helm. I took a moment to lean against the mast, closing my eyes in anticipation. It was finally happening. My excitement grew moment by moment. A short time later,

I stepped from the coach roof down into the cockpit next to my wife.

It took almost an hour to clear the outer point of the island. Without the obstruction of land, the wind was blowing much harder, about twenty knots.

"What perfect conditions," I said. "If it doesn't change, we'll have a downwind reach the entire way."

"Can't ask for better than that," she commented while vigilantly piloting our floating home up and over each ocean wave.

The sailing was fast and invigorating. We glided along at an easy six knots plus. After three hours of steady trade winds, the island of Utilla faded from view. Our anxiety grew. We both knew we were getting close. You could now see our next island destination off our bow. I checked and rechecked my waypoint on the GPS.

I took control of the helm as my wife snapped her safety harness to the jack line that ran fore and aft on the deck. She stepped up on the coach roof, holding onto the mast for support. This higher position gave her a much better view of the ocean ahead of us and any upcoming reefs and shoals. We would only get one chance at this.

"There it is," she screamed. "There it is; it's coming up fast."

A huge ocean swell rolled beneath us, raising the boat high and pushing us forward. *This is it,* I thought. *This is it.* I gripped the tiller tightly, took a deep breath and yelled a caution to my wife. "Hang on!"

THE DREAM

Dreams float in on wings of thought
As seeds that want to grow,
With knowledge plant these seeds as taught
Great gifts they will bestow.

Normally the water in this beautiful blue lagoon was calm but today it seemed agitated. Small wavelets and white caps danced across its surface. The Caribbean wind had been fickle all night. First it blew hard, then it calmed only to increase again. But for the last six hours it had blown at a steady twenty to thirty knots.

"Wind like this kicks up big waves, waves the size of freight cars," the captain said. "And waves that size will be breaking completely across the channel in the reef pretty darn soon."

The reef he spoke of was the barrier reef surrounding and protecting the island of Roatan, one of the Bay Islands located just off the coast of Honduras. The small natural cut was the only passageway to and from the large lagoon on the northeast side of the island. The lagoon was home to a small fleet of dive boats that sat moored safely to their docks. Standing next to the captain and the dive boats were all the divers anxiously awaiting the captain's decision. Will they go diving or not? His answer came quickly.

"There won't be any boats coming or going through that cut today. I'm sorry, folks, but I think it'd be far too dangerous. We better wait until tomorrow," he added.

Though everyone was a bit saddened by the decision, all could see his point. A quick glance out beyond the protected lagoon was all the validation needed. Giant waves pounded the barrier reef, sending white water and spume flying high into the sky. If you followed the reef line with your eyes, you could see the giant waves rolling through the cut. They weren't breaking yet, but you knew it was only a matter of time. And when they did, you sure didn't want to be trapped on the outer side of the cut trying to get back in. You'd be faced with the dangerous challenge of navigating such a small passageway into and through the cut in violent whitewater mayhem.

As the divers accepted the captain's decision, they dispersed to seek alternate activities for the day. Billy McCoy suggested to his wife, Dana, they walk over to the small café located on the beach just down from the dive shop. He figured they might as well have lunch.

That being the last day of their long-saved-for and long-awaited dive trip, Dana quickly agreed. And since they already had their swimsuits on, she suggested they spend the rest of the afternoon on the beach overlooking the beautiful blue lagoon. Having already had five wonderful days of diving, a day on the beach would be a fitting way to end their trip.

The couple walked the short distance to the café and found only two tables situated on the beach in such a way that the café itself blocked most of the wind. Each of the tables had two small wooden chairs set beside them. Both tables sat under the palm fronds of a single palapa. Since no one else was using either table, Billy and Dana settled in at the nearest and leaned back to enjoy the wonderful Caribbean view.

From where they sat at their table, the sandy beach stretched out about a hundred feet to the water's edge.

From the shore, the water gradually increased to about ten feet, then stayed pretty constant throughout the lagoon. The protected water was about six hundred feet wide and a half-mile long.

The barrier reef bordering the outer edge of the lagoon varied in width from ten feet at the narrowest to one hundred feet at the widest. Once beyond the reef, the floor of the Caribbean Ocean fell away quickly to thousands of feet in depth.

The waiter came and Billy and Dana placed their order.

Looking toward his wife, Billy spoke to her softy. "I know how concerned you have been lately, over money and all. But are you beginning to feel a little less anxious? I know we spent a chunk of our savings to pay for this trip. I really think we have good things coming. I was hoping you were feeling a little less stressed." He knew the answer to his question before he asked. He knew she wasn't feeling any better. He knew she was still worried. The uncertainty of what faced them when they returned home concerned her deeply. It concerned him too, but he felt the gamble was worth the strong possibility of success.

Dana looked affectionately at her husband and smiled. "We'll make it," she said, "we always do."

They both knew that was to be their last big expenditure for a while. With Billy's construction job coming to an end and the economy such that other work was scarce, they were seriously discussing the possibility of a move north. A move to the mountains of Colorado sounded great to both of them. Kind of like a new beginning. They had been able to save some money, enough for maybe six months, if they were careful. And even though they felt the change would do them good, both Billy and Dana were still very anxious. They were willing to stretch their money for a while. They knew they would have to, especially in light of Billy's new job offer, a sales job working for commissions only — no salary.

This is the part of the move that Dana feared the most: no guaranteed income. She was not the least bit excited about this new job offer. Billy knew the statistics. He knew more often than not, those who start a career in sales fail to become successful.

But, Billy thought, remembering the brochure that enticed him with the job in the first place, *those who work really hard patiently maneuver up the ladder of success and will be rewarded by a very prosperous career.* Billy felt confident in himself. So it was with this confidence and his reassurance that Dana agreed to move. Billy knew Dana still felt very tentative. He had hoped the dive trip would ease her mind.

Now, wanting to move their conversation to another subject, Billy looked out across the lagoon. Just as he was starting to comment on how the waves appeared even larger than before, he thought he caught a glimpse of something in the water, outside the barrier reef. "What's that?" he said, pointing out to sea.

He strained to focus his eyes, staring toward the last sighting in case the object appeared again. Billy held his hands above his eyes to screen out the bright sun.

"There it is again," he said, quickly pointing toward the object as it rose on a wave into view. "Do you see it?" he asked Dana. "What do you think it is?"

The object appeared to be something white floating on the water. It would appear high on a wave and then drop down again, out of sight.

"Maybe it's some kind of small fishing boat. Or maybe it's a buoy," she responded. "It appears to be floating on the water. Though it is a funny shape for a ship or a buoy. I just can't tell for sure."

"It's a sail," Billy exclaimed with confidence when he thought he figured it out. "It's the sail on a sailboat."

"Yes," Dana said in agreement, "I think you're right." She returned her gaze toward the small sailing vessel bobbing up and down in the massive ocean waves. Now she could see it clearly. The idea of it being a sailboat made it much easier to identify its shape and size.

"It appears to be three or four miles outside the reef, don't you think?" she questioned. At such a distance, it was still hard to differentiate between the white sail of the boat and the breaking white crests of the huge ocean waves.

"Yes," Billy agreed. "It's still a long ways out there."

The sight of the sailboat bouncing in such huge seas had his mind captivated. He was filled with questions. *What must the people on that little sailboat be experiencing right now? Surely, they have to be scared and desperate, sailing in conditions like this. Where did they come from? How many people are on the boat?*

Knowing nothing about sailing, the only image Billy had about sailboats involved white sails, sandy beaches, blue oceans, palm trees and tropical islands.

Billy smiled at himself when he realized those were the exact features of Roatan: sandy beaches, blue oceans, palm trees and a tropical island.

"Maybe the sailboat is coming here," Billy stated. "I wonder just how difficult it would be to safely maneuver a sailboat in waves like those. I bet it must take a lot of guts, as well as skill," Billy suggested to Dana, letting his imagination drift into the possibilities. "I wonder if they're coming to this island or just passing by."

"I don't know, but if they are coming here, I hope they know about the barrier reef," Dana said with concern.

"I sure hope they do," Billy responded.

Just then, the waiter came with their food. Their attention turned from the sailboat to their grilled fish sandwiches and punch drinks. They were enjoying 'the good life' in the tropical island paradise.

After a few moments, Billy finished his meal. He clasped his hands behind his head and leaned back in his chair. Suddenly, he lurched forward, screaming to Dana, "Look, look, there it is!"

"There what is?" she returned, jumping abruptly.

"The sailboat," he said. "It's already here. And it looks like it's going to sail into the lagoon through the cut. Dana, look at the waves now," he said, referring to their increased size.

"Impossible," Dana responded. "The waves are huge. They're breaking all the way across the cut."

They watched the sailboat for a few more minutes as it tacked back and forth outside the reef system. Now, with the boat being so close, Billy could see it wasn't such a small sailing vessel after all. Instead, it looked to be around fifty feet in length. As they both watched it maneuvering into position, Billy marveled at its flowing lines and symmetry. He loved the way the sleek boat sliced through the water with such grace and power. *It is a nautical marvel,* Billy thought. *The boat is beautiful.*

Watching intently, Billy noticed something. He observed the waves coming in sets, consisting of four or five individual waves. They marched into the cut in unison, breaking fiercely. Then there would be a lapse in action for a matter of forty-five seconds or so before the next set of waves. It was Billy's bet the sailboat skipper realized this, too. Billy figured the skipper was trying to time his entrance through the cut during the slack between the sets.

Leaning forward, Billy explained his theory to Dana. "It just might work," he told her. "It just depends on how fast that sailboat can pass through the cut in the reef."

As the current set of waves broke fiercely in the cut, the sailboat maneuvered forward behind them. The cut in the reef was only thirty to forty feet wide and was at least fifty feet in length, so it would be close. Not only did the skipper need to enter the small opening, he also needed to reach the inside edge of the cut before the next set of waves arrived.

"This is going to be close," Dana stated nervously, standing beside the table.

"I have my fingers crossed," Billy said anxiously, standing beside her.

Fortunately, the skipper's precision was good; having hit the entrance to the cut perfectly the graceful sailboat charged through the water like a racehorse. Quickly, the sailing yacht slid through the cut. Then, just as it was passing the inside edge, the next set of waves arrived. Huge mounds of water rose high behind the charging sailboat, threatening to break full force upon her stern. Just as the sailboat cleared the inner edge of the reef, the skipper tacked the boat hard to the right and furled the headsail, all at the same time. The sailboat cut in behind the reef's protected barrier and slowed. The next set of massive waves crashed and churned their way through the opening, but the sailboat was now out of their reach. It was safe.

Without the big headsail pulling, the boat maneuvered under the power of the mainsail alone. Slowly the sailboat made its way toward the inner shore of the lagoon.

"They made it, they made it," Billy and Dana danced around the table, singing to each other. Then they stopped briefly looking to see if anyone else was watching the excitement. But there was nobody else around. They were the only audience to such a perfectly timed feat. They both clapped and sat down quickly before anyone noticed their antics.

"What a show," Dana said. "I kind of feel tired from just watching. It was simply amazing. What skill they must have."

Billy nodded in agreement. He was impressed, to say the least. *What a beautiful sailboat and what a masterful crew*, he thought to himself. Billy was intrigued. Seeing this bit of adventure captured his mind, filling it with thoughts of possibility. *What a great and adventurous life it must be on the sea.*

The sailboat was close enough now that Billy and Dana could see the dark blue color of its hull. It moved slowly in their direction. The sailboat was working its way into the calmest portion of the lagoon, which happened to be just off the beach where Billy and Dana sat.

While still about one hundred feet beyond the water's edge, the sailboat turned back into the wind. This maneuver spilled the wind out of the mainsail, slowing the boat thus allowing it to drift to a stop. The person on deck dropped a huge anchor off the bow and fed a pile of chain out behind it. The skipper, still standing at the helm, turned the wheel hard, filling the mainsail full of wind again. This forced the boat to back down against the pile of chain stretching it tightly between the boat and the anchor. The wind pulled the boat so hard that it dug the anchor into the sand, securing the boat in place. She was safe now. As the boat straightened to the wind, they released the mainsail and it fell to the boom and the boat sat quietly in the calm lagoon.

Billy and Dana could see there were two people on the sailboat. They moved around on the deck, apparently tidying up the sails and various lines. Then they went below for a few moments only to return wearing swimsuits and holding a backpack. They eased themselves into the water by stepping down a boarding ladder they positioned off the stern of the boat. Then, holding the backpack high above his head, the skipper swam toward shore using one arm and both legs. Finally, making their way to shallow water, they both stood and walked hand in hand onshore.

The couple made their way toward the only other table on the beach. It happened to be set right next to Billy and Dana's table. Over the last hour, Billy and Dana had become somewhat emotionally involved with the sailing couple and their adventure. And yet, the sailors had no idea.

"Is this table taken?" the skipper asked, looking toward Billy.

"No, no," Billy blurted out. "Please, have a seat."

"Thank you," he said. "My name is Jack and this is my wife, Lucy."

"Billy McCoy, here, and my wife, Dana," Billy returned.

"You guys are our heroes," Billy furthered. "My wife

and I have been watching you for over an hour. You've been out there sailing in those huge waves. Wasn't it rough out there? How did you thread that small entrance into the lagoon? Now, here you are seated right next to us. You both act like it was just another walk in the park. We've been watching in fear for your lives with visions of your boat smashing into the reef. I just can't believe you're actually here."

Jack laughed as Billy's rambling slowed, but didn't stop. "An hour ago you looked to be a small sailboat miles offshore. Now you're two real people sitting right next to us. And," Billy continued with emphasis "what appeared from a distance to be a small bouncing sailboat now looks like a beautiful and graceful sailing machine of some fair length? It's just amazing, that's all."

"Well, I wish I'd known the two of you were paying such close attention to our entrance, I would have tried to make it look a little less sloppy," Jack responded. "Hope we didn't upset your plans by not crashing into the reef or getting caught by the waves while sailing through the cut," he said jokingly. "It was a bit bumpy out there. *Mana Loa*, our sailboat, is pretty tough. She handles the waves just like she was designed to. She was specifically built for offshore sailing. As far as the cut is concerned, it was marked on our chart and crossing through it was just a matter of timing.

"Where did you come from?" Billy asked Jack.

"We just sailed in from Jamaica. The trip took seven days," Lucy responded.

"Jamaica," Dana exclaimed. "That must be over a thousand miles from here. How long do you plan to stay in

Roatan? Where will you sail to next?"

"Well, we don't know the answer to either of those questions," Lucy said. "We will be here until we're ready to move along I guess. Then we'll go wherever we choose at that time. Hopefully it will be someplace new. We love sailing into countries we have never visited before."

"Wow, what a wonderful life," Dana said. "You sail around the Caribbean Ocean, make new friends and see new places, all with the power of the wind. What freedom that must be. Our lives, on the other hand, are full of kids, career changes and moving plans, just the opposite of yours."

"All in time," Lucy countered, obviously picking up on Dana's anxiety. "You're much younger than we are. Our kids are grown and our careers complete, so we decided to go sailing for a while. Jack's father was a sailor, so Jack had it in his blood. When we get homesick, we put *Mana Loa* in a safe marina and we fly home. We normally plan our trips back home to last a couple of months, but we usually miss this life so much, and of course *Mana Loa*, that we're back within a few weeks. She's become such a friend we hate to leave her alone for very long. We know she gets lonely when we're gone. Still, we do love our time at home with family and friends. The summertime out west is so beautiful."

"Well, that's where we are thinking of moving, out west to the mountains," Dana told them, still infatuated with Jack and Lucy.

"You guys definitely have an idealistic life. It's one that anyone would dream of," she continued, now sounding even more envious. "And you don't look that much older than we are."

"Jack had a short, but very successful career," Lucy responded. "We have been very fortunate. Our business life now consists of Jack flying home once a quarter for the board meeting with his family's corporation." When Jack's father stepped down as chairman of the board, Jack was voted in. At first, he didn't accept the position because he wanted to go sailing and didn't want to be tied down to a job. However, through the urging of his father and the promise by the board that his involvement would be limited to weekly email updates and his attendance at the quarterly board meetings, Jack accepted."

"Well, if you must have a job, that sounds like a great one to have, running the family business from the cockpit of your sailboat anchored in the clear waters of some island in the Caribbean Ocean," Dana stated, emphatically still not believing these guys' good fortune.

"Well, on the surface it does seem like a dream come true and we have much gratitude for our life. However, the dream of owning a successful corporation that in turn owns and directs several smaller companies was Jack's father's dream. It wasn't Jack's," Lucy told her. "Jack moved away from the family business twenty years ago. His interest wasn't in running a major corporation. His interest was in something much simpler. Something more grassroots and something that to him was far more rewarding, personally."

"Well, whatever his career was in, it appears to have served him well," Dana furthered, as she looked toward Billy, humorously suggesting with a smile. "You might look into a career like Jack's, Billy."

Billy looked at his wife. "Maybe I should," he responded with a gleam in his eye. "Maybe I should."

Now, their curiosity killing them, they both looked toward Jack with the same question, but Dana asked it first. "If you don't mind my being nosy, what was your career in?"

Jack nonchalantly looked toward Dana and replied. "I don't mind at all. I was in sales; I was a salesman."

Jack's answer took them both by surprise. It was not the answer either one expected, but especially not Dana.

"Sales," Billy said, feeling a charge of energy move through his body.

"Yes," Jack continued. "I like the one-on-one contact with my customers. I guess for me that was as rewarding as the income it produced."

"As Dana mentioned earlier," Billy responded, "we are planning a move. I have been offered a position in a sales office and I am considering taking it. One of my life's dreams is having a career I love, working the hours I choose while being rewarded financially for my performance. It sounds like a sales position can offer that. I have friends back home who have sales careers in different fields: real estate, insurance and such. They love it and do very well for themselves, but the commission-only part adds a bit of uncertainly to it."

"Well," Jack responded. "As a retired salesperson speaking to someone entering a sales career, I will say this: it is a noble and very necessary occupation. Without salespeople, our economy would quickly grind to a halt. You seem to have a pretty clear vision of what you want. If a successful sales career is your dream, don't get overwhelmed by the challenges you will face. Remember, boldness and commitment to your desire opens doors of opportunity you never expect and more often than not, they come when you least anticipate. I'm sure that's something you will experience personally. If you hold fast to your dreams, they will come true. Here's something else to keep in mind. It is far more important to know WHAT your dream is than to know HOW it will come to be. I wish you prosperity and good fortune."

The waiter came and Jack and Lucy placed their order. Billy and Dana left and quietly walked down the beach. All the while, Billy stared at the beautiful sailing vessel anchored just offshore.

"This is a life I would love to have," he finally said to his wife. "What do you think?"

"I can see us living this life. Who wouldn't love it?" she responded.

Billy smiled, "I can see it, too. What a dream!"

2

THE SALESMAN

It's through desire your dreams are born
Though distant they may seem,
Empower them and they will form
According to your dream.

From Billy and Dana's chance meeting with Jack and Lucy, their fear of a career in commission sales waned for the moment. They both seemed more hopeful of the possibility of a successful career, especially Dana.

Still, in the back of their minds they knew their family and friends thought differently; they were very skeptical. They felt the small amount of money Billy and Dana had saved would not last long. A sales job such as the one Billy was accepting didn't appear to offer much stability. "We'll see you in six months," they said, assuming Billy and Dana would fail at their attempt at a new life in Colorado.

Even though Billy and Dana heard the comments and their own fear and anxiety grew in response, they continued with their plans. A week after returning from Roatan, they loaded up their belongings and made the move to Colorado with their two small children. They soon found that being such a long way from home while trying to begin a new career actually brought the couple closer together. Both were dedicated at making the move work; they stuck to their minimum budget the best they could.

Their car was a twelve-year-old hand-me-down station wagon. Their home was a very small, below ground level apartment unit. Billy's business clothes consisted of a couple of cheap suits. But their hopes and expectations were high. Billy truly felt he had found the career he was destined for. Having the ability to set his own schedule meant a lot to him, though at that point in his career, it didn't mean more time off because being new in the business, he pretty much worked all the time. Billy really was dedicated to finding the success he and Dana had hoped for.

Every day he left for the office early; while there he watched the other salespeople make calls and work on proposals. Billy tried to emulate their actions.

Each day he watched as the names of the other salespeople went up on the sales board announcing their success from the prior day's activity. As he watched, Billy's determination grew in intensity. He couldn't wait for the day his name was up on the board. He dreamed of it being in top position. Billy knew that day was coming; he just had to keep at it.

But the long days passed and turned into weeks. Ninety days into his new career, his sales had been very few. The family's savings continued to dwindle. Billy's constant concern about their situation inspired him to work even harder and longer hours.

How much more effort can I put into this? he thought. *It already seems as though I work all the time.*

But undaunted, he continued. He re-memorized the sales presentation exactly as he was taught for what seemed the tenth time. Dana sat patiently listening late into the night as Billy practiced it over and over.

Billy relentlessly prospected for new customers and was always prepared whenever a sales opportunity presented itself. But still, the success he was looking for never came. He only made a sale here and there. There was no consistency.

There must be something wrong, he concluded, but what, he didn't know. He knew it couldn't just be bad luck. As the weeks went by, Billy's fear of failing ran rampant in his thoughts. It was just what his family and friends predicted. Everyone back home told him and Dana running off to Colorado was a poor decision, especially for the uncertainty of a sales job. Their lack of support was the last thing the young couple heard the day they left. And the thought of crawling back home in defeat was almost unbearable. That fear had been the reason Billy worked so hard. He figured if he didn't succeed, it would not be from lack of trying.

Billy continued to work hard even though his mind was plagued by his fears. Then one night five months after their move to Colorado, he and Dana were both looking up toward the ceiling as they lay in bed. The lights were off. Even in the darkness, Billy could feel his wife's worry and concern. It seemed to emanate everywhere. It was a sad time for them both. They weren't just worried anymore; the worry was nearing a panic level. They were almost out of money. Billy's successful sales career had not materialized. They both knew their dream was nearing its end.

"Maybe we should just go home," Dana suggested. "We have tried and tried. Our savings are almost gone. I know my folks would let us move in with them, until you find another job. I don't think we have a choice, Billy. We just can't hold on any longer. I think going home is our last and only hope."

Billy could tell by the sadness in her voice that Dana was suggesting something she really didn't want. She simply felt trapped and out of options, and so did he.

They both loved the mountains and the dream they shared of living in Colorado. The move had given them a feeling of independence. To move back now would make them feel defeated. Their dream would be lost. It would also be embarrassing to admit they failed. But it appeared to be their only choice. The fact was their money was gone. The small bit left would not even cover that month's rent. Billy's sales career appeared to be coming to a premature, and in some way, a predicted end; at least, predicted by their families.

Hours later, sleep finally came to the couple as they held each other.

Billy awoke the next morning a bit earlier than Dana. There was a tight feeling in his stomach. It hurt and felt unsettled. Whether it was caused by nervous tension, lack of sleep or whatever else, Billy didn't know. He just knew he didn't like the feeling.

In the beginning, Billy expected to make thousands and thousands of dollars. However, as time passed, his expectations changed. Billy simply wanted to earn at least enough money to feed and house his family.

The longer Billy lay there, the more he realized his feelings of sadness were changing into feelings of anger — downright anger.

Everyone in the office had been very helpful. There was always someone there to answer any question he had. It wasn't their fault he closed so few of his sales interviews. On the surface, it appeared he was doing the same as every other salesperson in the office. But for some reason success just wasn't coming his way.

As Billy lay there a bit longer, and the anger feelings subsided, a thought popped into his head. *Maybe, just maybe, there was another option, an option we haven't considered.* In Billy's mind, he felt so close to turning this career around. He didn't know why he felt this, but he did. This confidence was the reason they moved to Colorado in the first place. He just couldn't give up. He wished he had a little more time; he knew he could make this career work.

As Dana awoke and rolled in Billy's direction, she looked up at her husband. He smiled at her and tried to say something profound and encouraging, but all that came out of his mouth was, "I need three more months. It's not so long, Dana," he continued, not giving her a chance to respond. "How can we stay for three more months? I just know I can make this work. I feel I am so close and I really don't want to give up yet. If we give up now, I will never get another chance at this. If I can make this work we can have the life, here in Colorado the way we dreamed."

Dana lay there looking at her husband for a moment. She smiled then nodded in agreement. "I want this life too. And ninety days is not such a long time," she said. "But, as we know, it has been an uphill battle, with no end in sight. And even with all our desire to make this work, we are still out of money. But I've been thinking about this and have a suggestion." Dana had lain awake the night before for several hours trying to work out some kind of plan and she had one in mind.

"The kids and I need to go home for awhile. That will take some pressure off you. We can live with my parents until"…here her voice faded away. "For no more than three months," she stated emphatically.

"You will have to speak with the apartment manager and promise them we'll leave the place clean and perfect. And we will eventually cover the rent if they can't re-lease it. You will have to find a place to stay with one of your friends, I guess. Do you know anyone you might be able to stay with?"

Billy nodded affirmatively. "I think so," he said.

"And," Dana continued, this time with her finger pointing directly at Billy, "three months, period! Promise me if you have not caught up completely in our debts and re-established our savings, equal to at least another six months of income, YOU WILL COME HOME! We will have given this career its fair shot. I don't want to live any longer than that without you. You can find some other type of work. Do you promise me that?"

Billy knew it was a tall order. Getting the family caught up on the small amount of debt was the easy part. Six months of advance monies in the bank was something else. But what did he have to lose? It was his last shot and he intended to take it. Billy leaned down and kissed Dana on the forehead. "I promise," he whispered. And so it was settled. Billy and Dana had a plan.

The rest of the morning was busy, really busy. The kids were running around the house as Billy and Dana readied things for the move. Where they would store all the furniture and household goods they didn't know just yet — probably a storage unit. The kids knew something was up and kept asking questions about what they were doing. Both kids were still under six and found great fun in all the boxes and the chaos. It was different for Billy. Each time he passed Dana in the hallway, his stomach knotted up. He felt defeated. He felt as though he was losing his family, even though he knew it was just for a few months. He felt a great loss.

Billy felt totally to blame. If only he had succeeded, his family would not be leaving. Under the circumstances, failure was the prevailing thought in his mind — failure and sadness.

Later that day, Billy contacted one of his friends at the office. He spoke to him about their situation. His friend was single and lived alone in a three-bedroom home, not far from Billy's apartment. He immediately offered a bedroom and half of his garage to Billy. He even agreed to meet Billy the following day and help them with the move. Billy insisted on paying a certain amount of rent, but his friend refused. Though for the moment, Billy couldn't be too persistent; he didn't have the money then anyway. But Billy insisted on paying him as soon as he could. His friend finally agreed and they had a deal. It helped Billy to know at some point he would repay his friend for his kindness. Just knowing they had a place for their stuff and he had a place to stay made things seem much brighter.

Two days later after the move was complete, it was time for Billy's family to leave. Fortunately, Dana's folks decided to purchase airline tickets for her and the kids. They all loaded into the old station wagon and Billy drove them to the airport.

On the way, he tried his best to believe his family was taking a short vacation. But the closer they got to the airport, the more he felt his feelings of loss welling up inside. Once there, Billy pulled into the airport parking lot and found an open space. He looked at Dana and saw her tears. Then the kids began to cry once they realized Billy wasn't going with them. The idea of three months apart had no meaning to young children. What was important was that their daddy wasn't coming on the plane. It didn't seem right. The emotion of the moment is all it took. Billy broke down and released his pent-up anguish. All four cried as they held each other over and around the car seats.

"I promise to see you guys within three months and we'll be together again," Billy assured them. "Daddy has some things he has to do, then he'll come get you."

The family slowly made their way into the terminal. Dana and the kids passed through the checkpoint and loaded onto the plane.

Billy watched from the parking lot as the plane took off. His tears stopped, but the emptiness and tension in his stomach didn't. The feeling would stay with him, as a constant reminder of his family's separation. And it did something else. It seemed to fuel his effort toward success, and his NINETY-DAY promise.

The day after Billy's family left, he was up early and on his way to the office. Having made the decision to be up front and honest with his sales manager, Billy intended to tell him of his situation and the three-month time limit he was now working under. He wanted his manager to know he was willing to accept any assistance or advice he could offer.

The sales office he was employed by did a weekly mailing to a prospective customer list. This mailing always produced a few responses or lead cards. His manager would hand the leads out in an orderly fashion, trying to be fair with all the salespeople in the office. This was a good source for the company's business. But, of course, most of the business was developed by the individual salespeople and their efforts at prospecting for new customers through telephone calls, personal pre-approach letters, referrals and cold calls.

When Billy walked through the office door, he noticed his manager sitting in his private office, alone. He stepped up to the office secretary and asked if he could speak to the manager. Smiling, the secretary nodded affirmatively, motioning toward the manager's office.

"Good morning," Billy said, sticking his head into the opened door of the private office. "I hope I'm not bothering you. I was wondering if I might speak with you a minute?"

His manager looked up from what he was reading and motioned for Billy to enter and have a seat in the chair in front of his desk.

"Mr. McCoy, what can I do for you today?" he questioned, being very much straight to the point. Since Billy had attended all the sales presentation classes, as well as any other meetings offered to the salespeople, his manager knew him by name. But one-on-one conversation between the two of them had been few.

The office employed over thirty salespeople and his manager recognized them all, at least by name and approximate employment date. There were far too many for him to spend much time with each personally. When he did speak with one of them, he had a way of making them feel very much like they were his only salesperson. He appeared to have a genuine desire to help each one succeed.

"I just felt compelled to bring you up to date on my situation," Billy answered. "Things haven't been going very well for me. Yesterday, I had to put my family on a plane back home to live with my wife's parents. We are giving up our apartment. I moved in with a friend. I am trying to get my sales career moving forward. As you probably know, I have been employed here for going on six months. I have closed very few sales, though I have been on many sales appointments. I spend hours each day calling prospects and trying to fill my day with appointments. When I rotate up for your sales leads, I treat them with kid gloves and try my very best. In all honesty, the few sales I have made have been from the leads your office has shared with me. I think what I'm trying to say is my wife and I have agreed, if I can't get my feet on the ground and our savings built back up within three months, I'll have to terminate my employment and move back home. Our reserves are exhausted. I thought you should know." Billy was quiet now, awaiting a response.

His sales manager was a wise man. He knew how hard this young salesperson had been trying. The manager was in the office area as much as Billy was. He saw Billy's efforts and he really wanted to help.

The delay in the manager's response made Billy a bit nervous. He feared there was nothing more the manager could do. The manager had said, "Hard work should always prevail." Well, Billy felt he had been working hard and it was not prevailing, at least not so far.

Finally his manager spoke. "I am sorry for your situation, Billy. It was also very hard for me when I got started in my sales career. Six months is not a long time; sometimes it might take a year or even longer."

"I remember you explaining that to me before I started working here," Billy confirmed. "But I guess I really felt six months would be more than enough time to get my career started. Dana and I had six months of our projected income needs saved. It's all the money we had. We made the decision to give it a try. So far though, that has not proven to be such a good decision."

The sales manager continued staring at Billy. He knew how dedicated this young man was. He looked down at the lead cards on his desk.

"Well, let's look and see what we have here," he said, picking up the cards he was looking at when Billy first came into his office. "It looks like our last mailing was very successful," he offered. "Let's take the five leads from the top of the stack," he furthered, setting the other leads off to the side of the desk.

"All five of these look good," he noted, thumbing through them. "But," he said, allowing his voice to trail off. "This one looks especially good. I know this name, Yanis Barton. Yanis Barton owns the large farm just outside of town, off Powers Blvd. Barton Farms, I think it is. I hear he is a very, very successful man. Do you know who I'm referring to, Billy?" his manager asked.

"Well, I don't know Mr. Barton personally, but I have heard of the Barton Farms," Billy returned.

"Why don't you take these five leads and do your best, son," the manager suggested, handing Billy the lead cards. "I'm sure your time is near, just keep trying. Get back with me on Mr. Barton. I'd like to know how you did with him."

With that, the manager looked back toward the other leads and various papers on his desk. Billy thanked him for the help. He left his manager's office and went into the general sales area.

Billy felt different about these leads He didn't know

for sure just what it was, but he felt this just might be a real opportunity. Five leads were more than Billy had ever gotten at one time. This could be the start he'd been waiting for.

That afternoon Billy was very cautious and deliberate about making contact with the leads he was given. So far, the first two calls yielded two appointments for that evening and the next two calls got no answer.

Having saved what he thought might be the best for last; he looked at the number on the card that had Yanis Barton's name. Crossing his fingers, he dialed the number. Billy was nervous about this call, even though he had made many calls to prospects before. After the third ring, there was an answer.

"Hello, Barton Farms," the voice replied. It was a lady's voice.

"Hello," Billy said, making his introductions. "Is Mr. Yanis Barton available?" Short and to the point, that's what he'd been taught about using the telephone.

"No, he's outside right now. I'm sure he's in his woodshop," the voice replied.

Well, Billy knew leaving his number and asking for a return call had a low percentage of success. The best thing to do was explain that he would call again. The last thing Billy wanted to do was mess up this lead.

Before he could respond further, the voice continued. "May I help you? I'm his wife, Elizabeth Barton."

Here we go again, Billy thought. He knew if he told her about the lead, she may just say, "Oh, we're really not interested or something like that." Especially since the lead actually came from her husband. She probably knows nothing about it.

Well, Billy knew he'd better hurry up and say something before she hung up. *Honesty, honesty, honesty,* Billy thought to himself. *That's always best. I'll just be honest.*

"My company received a request from Mr. Barton," Billy quickly responded, then continued. "Mr. Barton asked for some information. I was calling to set a time to come by and bring the information to him." Billy crossed his fingers, hoping for a positive response. This was always a vulnerable point in calling for appointments.

"Well, I'm sure if he sent in a request for something, the sooner he gets it, the better," she responded in a matter-of-fact tone.

"Why don't you come by the farm? I'll step outside to the barn and tell him your coming. He'll be ready for tea soon, anyway. "But," she continued, "come before 2:00 o'clock, he naps around then." With that, Mrs. Barton hung up, never giving Billy a chance to respond.

Billy knew he'd gotten lucky. "Come on to the farm," was her comment. Billy shook his head, repeating her words. He was thankful not to hear the normal questions trying to qualify or justify an appointment. It was cut and dry. Mr. Barton requested it; he must want it. Billy checked his watch. It was eleven a.m. He had better hurry.

As quickly as he could get to his car, Billy McCoy was on his way to Barton Farms and Yanis Barton.

3

THE FARMER

You first must plant the seed in thought
Its image clearly see,
This clears the pathway dreams are brought
Into reality.

Yanis Barton stood over a thirty-foot-long piece of
Honduran teak wood. It measured only six inches
in height and two inches in width. The entire length
of wood was supported by fifteen waist-high sawhorses.
He'd created such a long piece of teak by fitting three smaller
lengths of wood together using clamps. Having just finished
shaping and smoothing the edges, he stood back, admiring his work. Looking at it from every direction, he slowly
walked back and forth from one end to the other. Slowly he
ran his fingers along its full length, feeling for any imperfection. Finally, he was satisfied.

Yanis smiled, looking at what was to be one of the
two new caprails for his old classic L. Francis Herroschoff,
H-28 sailboat. The sailboat sat in a cradle in the protection of
his boat barn. Yanis had already removed all the paint from

the deck, the topside and hull. Then having smoothed and re-faired her wooden sideboards, he'd painted her completely with a gray water-retardant primer. She would soon be ready for the professional painter to give her the final color coats. Without her final paint, she almost looked naked, like a gray ghost.

Even in her unfinished condition, Yanis loved her. *What a magnificent piece of naval architecture*, he thought. Her hull had been designed in 1936. More of her sister ships had sailed around the world than any other sailing vessel built. *Someday, I'll have her ready to once again sail the world's oceans*. Yanis smiled at his own thoughts, knowing her sailing days with him were over. He was glad he would get her back into near-perfect condition. In some ways, she would be even better than the original. But the ocean would probably never see this old girl's grace and charm again. She would take her place along the wall with Yanis' collection of old-world sailing vessels. Yanis himself was an old classic, destined never to sail again.

He turned his gaze toward the other side of the barn. Positioned along the entire one hundred feet of its length was his collection of old vintage sailboats, ten in all. One from each of the naval architects, he most admired. Architects and their creations like Olin Stevens and his Tartan 34, Carl Alberg and his Alberg 30, Phillip Rhodes and his Swiftsure 33 and Van de Stat and his Trintella 29, just to name a few. He stood there marveling at each masterpiece. He wondered where they had sailed. What oceans had they crossed? What storms had they endured? What islands had they seen?

Yanis stood there admiring each of the restored beauties when he heard a voice. Even at his age of eighty-six, his hearing was still very good. He knew it was his wife, Elizabeth, who he had been married to for sixty-two years. As he turned toward his very petite wife with long, straight silver hair, who was eight years younger than he was, Yanis' eyes sparkled. She always made them sparkle. She had ever since the first day they met.

"I bet you brought me some tea," he said, smiling when he noticed the pot and two cups she carried in on a tray.

"Every day, 11:15 sharp, you know that," she said, motioning toward the two lawn chairs positioned by the door. "You've been at it pretty hard this morning. It's time to take a break. Oh, by the way, there's a man coming out to see you; he says you ordered information about something."

"Information?" Yanis responded, shrugging his shoulders. "I don't remember ordering anything. Well, no matter, I guess I'll remember when he shows it to me."

Elizabeth just smiled at her husband. He was very laid back. He took life with ease. Yanis enjoyed his life. His business life, his children and grandchildren, he cherished them all. But for the moment he was focused on his sailboats. Some of the boats had been with him for well over fifty years. He loved them as much now as he did when he first bought them.

Each boat was special to him. Yanis sailed each before it took its position along the wall, as he called it. Though each of the boats was unique in its own way, they had their similarities. "How's a man supposed to get in here to work on these things," he would say. "How did this hull paint get so scratched? Look, the new varnish is already peeling. This wench needs more grease. The stainless already needs some attention."

Yes, Elizabeth thought, *it may be a different boat, but it's always the same story. My husband may not stand as tall and be as strong as he was in his youth, but his passion for boats hasn't waned. And the memories of his joyful life adventures still flourish.*

In the driveway, Goose, the family's old English Pointer, started barking. Elizabeth leaned over, looking out the door of the barn. An older model station wagon pulled up in front of the house. Stepping out of the car, Billy McCoy walked up to the front door of the house.

"We're out here," Elizabeth called out the barn door. "We're out here in the woodshop."

Billy turned his attention toward the voice. Seeing Elizabeth seated in her lawn chair waving out the door, he walked in her direction, stopping only briefly to reach down and pet Goose. Goose, in turn, once satisfied there were no treats forthcoming, again took her vigilant watch position, laying in the swing on the front porch.

"Hi, my name is Billy McCoy," the young man said to the couple. He reached his hand out toward Yanis, who slowly stood to shake it.

"Yanis Barton," the old man said. "My wife, Elizabeth Barton," he continued motioning toward Elizabeth who stayed seated.

Elizabeth nodded and Billy did the same.

"You brought information for me?" Yanis asked, still not remembering what information he had asked for.

Billy didn't respond immediately. His focus was elsewhere. He stood quietly staring at the long line of sailboats that captured his attention. They were neatly lined up side by side with their bows pointing toward the center of the barn.

"Wow, what beautiful sailboats," Billy said, gesturing toward the restored beauties. "What graceful lines they have. They almost look like a pod of dolphins swimming in a straight line. They look like proper little sailing yachts. What are they doing here in Colorado?"

"You know something about sailboats?" Yanis questioned him, admiring the young man's obvious attraction to his collection.

"No, sir, not really," Billy told him. "But I did gain a fair respect for their ocean-going capabilities. A few months ago, I saw one sailing through some dangerous waves when my wife and I were on a dive trip in Central America. After talking with her skipper, I realized how much faith and confidence was placed on a sailboat's design and in its quality of construction. He indicated each boat was designed and built to perform the tasks intended. He said they developed their own distinct personality, almost like becoming part of the family."

"Well," Yanis responded to Billy, impressed with the young man's enthusiasm, "I would say you know more about sailing yachts than you let on. Your brief description of a sailboat is spot on. They each do possess a grace and personality of their own. That is something seldom realized, except by someone possessing a certain passion for them." Yanis led Billy down the row of sailboats. He stopped at each and gave a brief description of the boat's history, as he knew it. The two men were having great fun talking. The more Billy learned about sailboats, the more he wanted to learn, and Yanis was a wealth of knowledge and experience.

"People who see the sweetness of a boat's sweeping sheer line or the aggressive wave-parting angle of her bow, or the beauty of the long overhang in her stern design — in my mind they are boat people, Billy. They're kind of special," Yanis said, smiling broadly.

"Well, I guess I never thought of it that way," Billy said. "But I do see the beauty in each of these boats. Especially this one right here," he continued, pointing to the gray-hulled boat Yanis was still working on. "This one takes my mind away to distant islands and warm blue oceans."

"Oh yes," Yanis agreed proudly. "She is my baby. She is the sweetest of them all. She's not much to look at right now, but you just wait. I made a commitment to this boat long ago. I told her I'd put her back into shipshape and I intend to make that happen. She is my favorite. She's a Herroschoff designed, H-28."

"She is beautiful," Billy said. "I can only imagine what she'll look like all painted and complete."

"How old are you, son?" Yanis asked as he led Billy over to the side of the sailboat he was working on.

"I'm twenty-four," Billy said, wondering why Yanis would ask.

"Twenty-four, you say," Yanis whispered softly leaning toward Billy so Elizabeth couldn't hear him speak. "When I was your age, that would have been over sixty years ago, I sailed this boat," he reached over and affectionately touched the hull of his H-28, "thirty-three thousand miles around the world. It took me five years to do it. That boat right there got me home safe and sound through some terrible, terrible storms. She never let me down and I promised her I would make her look brand-new again. That's what I'm doing now, keeping a sixty-year-old promise."

"Around the world, really!" Billy exclaimed. "In that little sailboat? It looks so small!"

"Size means nothing," Yanis returned. "It's the design and how well it's built that counts. I bet more boats with that hull design have been sailed around the world than any other type."

"That must have been a real adventure," Billy responded, shaking his head in amazement. "I bet you have some great stories. Tell me one, Mr. Barton. What was your favorite story or your favorite experience during your trip?"

Yanis took a moment to think while he watched Billy closely. He nodded his head, acknowledging to himself that he really liked this young man, and it wasn't just because Billy showed such an interest in his boats. Yanis couldn't quite put his finger on it. But there was something about Billy that Yanis was attracted to.

Yanis did have a favorite story, but it was one he seldom shared with others. Yet, for some reason Yanis was inclined to share it now. *Maybe I could just tell Billy part of it,* he thought. *Yes, that's a good idea. That's what I'll do. I'll just tell him part of the story, no harm in that.*

"I have many stories," Yanis told Billy. "But I guess I do have a favorite one. It's the part of my voyage that made the most impact on my life."

"Then tell me that one," Billy urged.

"Well, there were two things in this story that changed my life forever," Yanis began.

But, just as he got started on his tale, Elizabeth stood up and walked over to where the two stood.

"Oh no," she said humorously. "Yanis is telling you one of his sailing stories, isn't he?" She smiled affectionately at her husband then turned toward Billy.

"Well, you boys have fun with your stories. I'm going to the front porch to sit in the swing with Goose. I'll check on you later. Don't let your tea get cold, Yanis." With that, Elizabeth left the barn.

"Around the world," Billy repeated again. "You sailed that boat thirty-three thousand miles, all the way around the world."

"Yes, I did," Yanis replied, now having a green light to talk all he wanted. He had somebody who really was interested in his sailboats, and his lovely wife gave him the go-ahead.

"I'm ready for that story, Mr. Barton," Billy said impatiently.

"Well," Yanis said, "I was sailing in the South Pacific Ocean down through the Marquesas Island chain when the two of us, me and the boat, were overtaken by a terrible storm." Yanis spoke as if the boat was an individual herself.

"The waves had grown so large they were breaking above the height of my spreaders." Yanis pointed to the cross supports on the mast that help hold the mast upright. They appeared to be about twenty feet above the deck of the sailboat.

"I had to steer her by hand because the speeds she reached surfing down the back of the monstrous waves made her rigging shake. I had to keep constant pressure on the tiller to keep her moving diagonally across the back of those giants. I knew I needed to 'hove to' and take the pressure off her rigging and give myself a break from steering. But I had a problem. I was too close to land. The island chain I was trying to claw away from was only a few miles off my stern. I realized that in these horrible conditions, we were making little outbound progress. All we could do was run a parallel course to the island. With the direction of the wind and the sea state, it was the only choice I had.

"If I 'hove to,' the wind and the current would take us straight toward shore. I knew she'd end up on a reef."

Billy looked a bit confused so Yanis explained. "'Hove to' is the process of back-winding the staysail or jib. Then, by easing the mainsail to spill all or most of the wind, the two sails counteract each other. If you hold the tiller in a negative position, it allows the boat to drift very slowly with the current keeping her bow in a favorable angle toward the oncoming waves. When executed properly, a 'hove to' boat will sit calmly, even in the fiercest seas."

After Yanis' explanation, Billy nodded and the old man continued, "At the speed we were sailing, I could tell we were making good headway toward the end of the island chain. Every time we crested the top of a monster wave, I could see the islands in the distance behind us. I was doing my best to sail down the waves at an angle to keep her from burying her bow into the next oncoming wall of water. It seemed an unrelenting task. By now, Billy, we'd been in the rough storm conditions for almost twenty-four hours. I was exhausted.

"At our current pace I figured it would take at least a few more hours to clear the last island in the chain. Then 'hoving to' would be a possibility. I vigilantly persevered and kept her going on our current heading.

"On and on we sailed. Slowly, but surely, we made headway. The hours continued to pass. I was getting more and more tired. My mind wandered from the situation when I noticed a small yellow bird fly up and land on the sheet line secured to the wench. It was trying to get out of the storm. I'm sure the wind had blown it out to sea from one of the islands. It was looking for anything to perch on and rest. But the little bird didn't stay on my sheet for long. Almost immediately, it hopped down into my cockpit. Then it flew down below, inside the cabin. I guess it really wanted out of the wind and rain. I didn't mind. In fact, I wished I could have done the same. But that wasn't in the cards for me."

"How could you physically steer a sailboat through the huge waves you describe for hours on end without collapsing?" Billy asked.

"The answer to that question, Billy, is I didn't," the old man said. "It must have been about four hours later. The sun had set and I was so exhausted, wet and getting scared. I remember how I kept talking to her. 'You can do it, Babe, you can do it.' I kept pushing her on and on.

"The pounding this old girl was taking was unimaginable. I just don't know how she held together the way she did. I knew we had to be close to clearing the island chain. If it had been daylight, I would have known for sure because I would have been able to see the islands behind us. But in the darkness, I couldn't tell exactly where we were. Billy, it was one of those really dark, dark nights, where there are no stars, just blackness everywhere.

"Suddenly I heard a noise that sounded like a freight train. Even though I couldn't see it, I immediately knew what it was. It was a giant rogue wave. I could feel it sucking the air from around me as it rose high above. Before I could react to this mammoth wall of water, it was on me in an instant. I pushed hard to port on the tiller, but the suction coming from the bottom of the wave was more than we could deal with. With all my might, I tried to force her bow to starboard, up the wave face. And just when I thought we had a chance to make it, she twisted on me. That powerful wave was just too much. As her bow slammed back to port, the boom flew the opposite direction and caught me standing high in the cockpit. I raised my arm to fend it off. The boom hit my arm with such force, it smashed my forearm. I immediately saw my broken arm and the bones sticking out of a four-inch gaping wound. It was then the boat took a lunge forward, throwing me backward. I hit my head on the wooden combing surrounding the cockpit. As I lay there, things got real quiet. I felt a cold chill. I could feel my consciousness fading. I knew I was hurt, but I couldn't do anything about it. All I remember saying before I passed out was, 'It's all up to you, Old Girl. I can't help you anymore.' Then all went black."

Yanis stood there quietly for a moment, not saying anything. He was wrapped up in his memory of that moment.

Billy was impatient. "Then what happened?" he urged. "What happened after you blacked out?"

"Well, Billy, honestly, I can't really say," Yanis responded, patting the hull of his old friend. "But I do know one thing for sure. This old girl saved my life. The last thing I remember is falling into unconsciousness in her cockpit during the fiercest storm we'd ever faced together. My last mental picture was my broken, mangled arm." Yanis raised his arm slightly for the dramatics of his story.

"Then," Yanis continued, "what I remember next is waking up. Everything was calm. The sun was high in the sky. The storm had passed. I was lying on a grass mat on the beach in the shade of a palm tree. Now, Billy, I think I need to sit down for a minute."

Yanis stepped over to the lawn chair and pushed it against the wall of the barn. He sat down and leaned his head back to rest.

"What are you guys doing out here?" came a voice from behind. It was Elizabeth coming back into the barn. "You two still out here talking about boats?"

"I guess we are," Billy responded, turning in her direction. "Mr. Barton was telling me a pretty good story. It was a story about when his H-28 saved his life."

"Really?" Elizabeth questioned with a surprised look on her face.

"Yes, Ma'am," Billy affirmed.

She turned toward her husband for further confirmation, but found him fast asleep.

"I guess he wore himself out with that story," she said, looking in Billy's direction. "He so enjoys talking with someone he feels has a certain appreciation for his boats. But that particular story he doesn't tell very often. It's a special story to him. And I know he would never tell it unless he felt you had 'something special.' So, I wonder?" Her voice trailed away. It was as if she was thinking something more, but unsure whether to say it or not. "Well anyway, Billy, did you ever speak with him about that information you brought?"

"Oh no, Ma'am, I forgot all about it," Billy said. "We got so wrapped up in talking about boats and all."

"I guess you did," Elizabeth said. "You have been at it for three-and-a-half hours. He usually takes a rest by two. I fell asleep in the swing with Goose. It's now three o'clock and I never even brought you two lunches. He must have really been having fun. He doesn't often get a chance to tell his stories anymore. Especially that story," she said again. "I'm still surprised he's telling it."

She stopped briefly to study the young man standing next to her, and then she continued, "Why don't you come by tomorrow, Billy? Come by earlier, maybe 8:30 or so, and have another go at it with him. I know he likes you and he would be thrilled if you returned. You can bring your information then."

Elizabeth moved the other lawn chair to sit beside Yanis.

"I'll just sit here with him for awhile," she told Billy. "You know," she continued as if questioning him. "If Yanis was really telling you the story about how his boat saved his life, he really must feel you are special. I can't remember the last time he told that story to anyone. Not since he shared it with our son, many years ago. You drive careful, Billy, and we'll see you tomorrow."

Elizabeth leaned her head against the wall of the barn and quietly sat beside her husband.

Billy left the barn and drove down the driveway toward Powers Blvd. The driveway was over two miles long. When he had come to the farm, he hadn't noticed the cornfields lining both sides of the driveway. *I bet all these cornfields are owned by Barton Farms,* he thought.

Billy had appointments that evening and needed time to prepare. But somehow he knew it had already been a very good day. Billy felt like he'd just made a very special friend. He almost felt at home with the Bartons.

Back at the office, Billy set about preparing himself for his appointments. While he worked, his mind drifted back to Elizabeth's comment. *What did she mean when she said Yanis must have thought I was special? And why was he telling me the 'special story' about his sailboat? Well, I guess I'll find out tomorrow. Right now, I have appointments to tend.*

That evening he made the two presentations quickly and effectively. He identified their needs, while clearly presenting his product as a logical and affordable solution. They both purchased. He left the appointments very happy. Billy was amazed at his good fortune. It was the first time he'd made two sales in one day.

As he was driving home that evening, he found himself again thinking about Elizabeth and Yanis. In fact, he realized he'd been thinking about them throughout both presentations. He felt lucky he even remembered his presentation at all. The two sales would help immensely. He was off to a good start.

When he got home, he called Dana. He was tired, but very excited and proud. It had definitely been a good day for Billy McCoy.

4

THE KAHUNA

The Ancients knew the inner force
That flows from deep within
As Mana Loa, and the source
Where all of life begins.

The next morning, Yanis was up at his normal time, six a.m. He had a new coffee pot that turned on automatically at a programmed time. He thought it was the greatest invention. Each evening Elizabeth set the coffeemaker to make coffee the following morning, knowing how much Yanis enjoyed getting up to already-made coffee.

That morning, like every morning, Yanis took his cup of coffee outside to watch the sunrise. He sat in the swing on the front porch next to Goose. In her day, she could point with the best of them. Squirrels, lizards, quail, crows or deer — they were all the same to Goose. Now she was up in years just like Yanis and Elizabeth. Most days she would lay around the porch guarding the driveway, in-between her naps. Periodically, she walked to the barn and checked on the boats or Yanis for something to do. But at dawn each morning, she sat on the porch with the Bartons as they greeted their day.

"Billy is coming back this morning," Elizabeth told Yanis. "He said you were telling him the story about how that sailboat saved your life. Is that true?"

"Yes, it is," Yanis replied hesitantly. "I didn't tell Billy the whole story, just the beginning. I don't really know why I decided to tell it to him, I just did. I have a feeling this boy is kind of special. I think he has the Kaula-O, as Alexander would say."

"I have to admit, Yanis, I like him too. It's not often I hear you talk that way about someone. The last time I remember you telling that story must have been to our son when he was a child. Is that right?"

"Yes, it is," Yanis said. "We'll see how things go today."

"Now, Yanis, let Billy tell you about himself," Elizabeth warned him. "Don't just jump right into boats and sailing tales. He has a story and you need to let him tell it."

"I will, I will," Yanis agreed, smiling as he finished his coffee. "Now, pretty please, can I go to the barn?"

"You're excused," she said like a stern schoolteacher.

By seven o'clock that morning, Billy was treating himself to a proper breakfast at one of the nicer diners in town. Usually, breakfast was a quick bowl of cereal and piece of toast, but today was special. He'd made two sales the night before. Two of the leads his sales manager had given him yesterday already proved successful. And each of those new customers referred some of their friends to Billy. Billy felt he was on his way. *This could be it,* he thought. *This could be the opportunity I've been waiting for.* Billy's hopes were high.

He finished breakfast and then looked at his watch. It was eight o'clock. A twenty-minute drive would have him at the Barton Farm just on time. He quickly paid the bill and left.

As Billy turned onto the driveway off Powers Blvd, he again noticed the acres and acres of corn on both sides of the drive. He also noticed there were no weeds in or around the rows, nor were there any weeds bordering either side of the drive. The green grass on both sides was cleanly cut and tidy.

Goose announced Billy's arrival. But she must have remembered the car from the day before because she stopped barking quickly and returned to her sentinel position on the swing for another nap.

Billy was just getting out of his car when Elizabeth stepped out of the house onto the porch. "Good morning," she said before pointing toward the barn with a smile. "Don't forget the information," she reminded Billy.

What a nice person, Billy thought. He was sure thankful he'd met the Bartons. He walked into the barn just as Yanis was taking the clamps off the new caprail.

"Hello," Yanis said as he looked up from his project. "Did you bring your work clothes?"

"These are my work clothes," Billy retorted. "I'm a salesman, remember?"

"That you are and a mighty fine salesman at that," Yanis replied. "Bring those two lawn chairs over here and let's sit a minute. I've been at this for over an hour already and I need a break."

"You're not going to fall asleep again, are you, Mr. Barton?" Billy questioned, sporting a big smile.

"Yesterday had been a long day. I must have been tired," Yanis grunted, shaking his head at Billy's humor. "Tell me about that information I requested," he continued, now sitting down.

Billy pulled out the lead card with Yanis' name on it. He handed it to the old man.

Yanis looked at the card. "I remember this," he said. "Is this for real? Can this thing actually do what it says?"

"Yes, it can," Billy responded quickly and emphatically. "The company guarantees your satisfaction or you get your money back."

Billy stood there. He was ready to follow up with more information when Yanis spoke.

"How many people return it and ask for their money back?" he asked.

"I don't know for sure, Sir. I have never had one of my customers return theirs."

Billy spoke the truth. He hadn't sold very many, but not one had been returned. Still, even though this was the truth, Billy felt a bit ashamed of his answer. He felt it was a bit evasive; not really the whole truth.

Just then, Elizabeth came into the barn. "I brought you boys a cup of coffee," she said smiling, carrying a tray with three cups and a pot of coffee. "Billy, can you grab the other chair just outside the door and bring it in?"

While Billy retrieved the chair, she asked Yanis, "What are you talking about in here, more boats?"

"You got here just in time to save me from this sharp and wily salesman," Yanis responded, handing the lead card to Elizabeth to review.

Billy thought the old man was joking with his comment, but quickly took a glance at him just to make sure. Yanis was smiling.

Elizabeth looked at the card. "I've seen these. One of my friends at bridge club has one. She absolutely loves it. She talks about it all the time. She's always telling me I need one."

"Well, that does it then," Yanis said in a booming voice. "If one of those social club biddies loves it, it must be good. Let's buy one. What do you say?" Yanis asked, looking in his wife's direction.

"You're right. I think we should. But, I'd also like to get one for Jim and Mary."

Now she looked at Billy to explain. "Jim is the foreman on our North End Farm. Mary is his wife. They're not just employees, they're very good friends."

"Then it's done," Yanis agreed. "We'll buy two."

Billy was beside himself. *They're buying two*, he thought. *I have to act calm,* he cautioned himself. *Don't act too excited. Stay calm.*

"Wait," Elizabeth interjected. "What about our other foremen? What about everyone else who works for us? Maybe it's not such a good idea to buy it for one employee and not for the others."

Billy stood there awaiting their decision. What they decided to do didn't really matter to him. He would be happy if he just sold them one. Anything more would be a bonus and it would still be a very good day.

Yanis thought for a moment. "You may be right. Here is an option," he said, looking at his wife. "Do you remember a while back when we were talking about trying to give all of our employees a really nice gift toward yearend?"

"I remember," Elizabeth responded, nodding her head affirmatively. "But we were talking about every employee in the company, weren't we?"

"Yes, we were — everyone," Yanis furthered. "I like these things and I think they'd make a great employee gift. It's been two very prosperous years for our company and I think we should do something special for everyone. I think this might just be it — the perfect gift. What do you think?"

Elizabeth loved her husband. He was such a kind old man. He was always coming up with ways to give back to people. This would cost the company a lot of money, but she knew Yanis didn't care. He enjoyed sharing his success. His employees were very important to him. They always had been.

"Yes," she said quickly. "I think that would be a fabulous idea. Every employee gets one."

Every employee, Billy thought, visibly beginning to shake. *They did say every employee. But how many employees did that mean?* He knew their farm was big. They probably farmed several thousand acres, Billy guessed. His mind was calculating the possibilities.

Stay focused, he thought. *Stay focused*. However many people Barton Farms employed, Billy would be grateful.

"I'm happy for your decision," Billy said, having to say something to try and calm his nerves. "I am sure your employees will be very happy also. I know they'll love your gift. How many employees do you have working on this farm?" Billy's guess was the farm employed four or five people. He was hoping so, anyway. *What a day this was going to be if that were the case*, he thought.

"Well," Elizabeth replied, tilting her head sideways while trying to count. "The number of employees working for the three sections of Barton Farms is fourteen."

"Fourteen," Billy blurted out, not controlling his emotions. "You have fourteen people employed at this farm?"

"The number of people employed by our three farm sections, total fourteen, yes," Elizabeth answered. "We farm over twelve thousand acres."

Billy was now really beginning to feel weak. They wanted fourteen, plus one for themselves. What was happening to him? How could this be? Wrapped up in a gush of emotion, Billy felt a tear running down his cheek.

A tear, he thought. *How could I have tears after such a stroke of good fortune? I should be jumping for joy, not shedding tears.*

Sitting next to Billy, Elizabeth noticed his emotion. Yanis didn't. She quickly changed the subject, trying to give the young man a few private moments.

"Yanis," she said. "Why don't you show me that new caprail you're making while Billy goes to his car and gets the forms he needs to place our order?"

Yanis stood up from his chair, curious as to his wife's sudden interest in his boat.

"So now you want to see my new caprail, do you? I'm pretty proud of it. Come over here and look at this masterpiece."

Billy was sure he saw a slight wink in Elizabeth's eye as she sent him to his car. She probably realized he had his briefcase lying right there on the floor next to him. *She is such a kind person,* he thought.

Billy accepted the moment gracefully, picked up the briefcase and walked to his car. Once outside the barn and out of sight of Yanis and Elizabeth, he stopped. He immediately noticed something. For the first time since his family left, two days earlier, the nervous tension he felt in his stomach was gone. Billy felt good. He sat in the car for a few moments and closed his eyes to let the feeling soak in. His mind was filled with joy. He felt such gratitude to his manager for sharing the lead with him. Billy also felt great affection for the Bartons. Not because they were making the purchase, but because they were wonderful people. He felt honored to have met them.

After calculating the cost for fifteen, Billy stepped back into the barn.

"All I need are the addresses of your employees for delivery purposes, your signature on this order form and a check for," he stuttered slightly at the huge number, "nine thousand dollars."

There, he thought, *he said it.* He slowly glanced toward Yanis and Elizabeth, hoping the figure didn't change their decision.

"Why don't you run and get our checkbook," Yanis asked his wife. "We'll pay for the Barton Farms order today and submit the total purchase request to the Company's Board of Directors for approval. They can reimburse us for the Barton Farms purchase after the board meeting. They don't meet until next month."

"Sounds like a plan," Elizabeth said, already on her way to the house for the checkbook.

Wonderful, Billy thought. *They still wanted the order. This is more than wonderful.* He was floating on cloud nine as he stepped over to where Yanis stood by his long piece of wood.

"Mr. Barton, you may never know how much I truly appreciate your trust and your business." With that, Billy reached out and shook the hand of the man who had just given him the start he'd been waiting for.

"Billy," Yanis replied. "Life comes at us from all directions. Sometimes we see it coming, sometimes we don't. Sometimes it seems good and sometimes maybe not so good. In this case, you had a product and I had a desire. You fulfilled my desire, and in so doing, maybe in part, I fulfilled yours. We both win. I would say we both created well."

"Come sit for a moment, son," Yanis continued almost in a fatherly way. "Tell me about yourself. Do you have a family?"

"Yes, Sir, I do," Billy responded. "I have a wife and two children. My son is five and my daughter is three."

"Then you have your hands full at home," the old man said.

"Normally I have a very busy life at home. Right now though, my family is living," Billy paused for a moment before he continued, "my family is visiting my wife's folks out of state. Things have been much quieter since they're away." Billy was speaking cautiously and slowly now. He was watching his words. His family situation was embarrassing to him. It wasn't something he wanted to share freely. So feeling a bit guilty for not being completely honest, he decided to change the subject.

Billy realized that for the second time that day, he felt as if he was hiding something from the Bartons.

Honesty, Billy thought, *honesty was the answer. Honesty without exaggerating is the right way to explain this. Besides, with this sale today, I am much closer to moving my family back.*

Billy knew honesty was the best direction. Especially in the case of the warranty he never completely explained earlier. If there was to be any possibility that would make a difference, he needed to know it now, before he counted the income from this huge sale.

"Mr. Barton," Billy said slowly. "I need to clear something up. You ask me earlier what percentage of clients returned their products to the company. I said I wasn't sure. I said none of my customers ever had. Both answers are the truth. I really don't know what percentage of people return the product. And I have never had anyone return one that I sold. What I didn't say was that I have only sold a few. I am new to the business and I am still trying to learn the ropes, so to speak. If you would like me to find out what the return percentage is, I will be happy to do that for you."

Having already accepted Billy's answer to the return question, Yanis didn't intend to pursue it further. And he noticed the brief change in Billy's comment about his family, but he didn't want to probe into that either. Yanis recognized and was very thankful for the honesty Billy displayed, especially in reference to the return percentage.

"It is not important," Yanis commented. "I'm sure the factory guarantee would not be offered if the product wasn't a good one.

Compassionately, Yanis moved onto something else. "Next step here is to attach the new caprail to the hull/deck joint of my H-28," he said, pointing to the long piece of teak sitting on the sawhorses."

"How are you going to lift that long piece of wood and set it in place?" Billy asked, glad the subject had changed. "It looks to me like it's too long to pick up in one piece."

"You're right," Yanis said. "But if you notice," he gestured, showing Billy the joints, "the long piece of wood is actually three smaller pieces. I haven't secured the joints with glue and sealant yet. If I take the long piece apart, I have three smaller pieces. All I have to do is set one small piece at a time,"

Billy took a closer look. "I see that now," he said.

"Need some help putting the rail in place? She's such a beautiful sailboat. I would love being a part of her restoration, even if it was just a small part."

Billy was sincere about that. He did want to help Yanis. And he did think the boat had the most beautiful lines of all the boats in Yanis' collection. It was as if its shape spoke to him.

Though Yanis and the sailboat distracted Billy for a moment, the excitement of the sale he'd just made was almost uncontrollable. He felt like he wanted to scream. He just couldn't wait to call Dana and share the good news. What would Billy's sales manager think when he reported back to him about Yanis Barton?

"I know you have things to do besides hang around here working on this old boat," Yanis told him, though he was secretly hoping Billy would stay. "But," he quickly continued, "I might let you help me with the first piece. It will be the most difficult. I would appreciate that."

"You're on," Billy responded immediately, stepping to the side to remove his tie and roll up his sleeves.

"But," Billy continued, "after we put this first piece in place, I sure would like to hear how you ended up on the beach. Remember the story? You did kind of leave me hanging."

Yanis smiled at Billy. "Yes, I do remember. I suppose a bit more of the story could be arranged."

Having already removed the side clamps, all they had to do was pull on each end of the long piece of wood and the joints separated, leaving three individual pieces.

Together they picked up the first ten-foot length of wood. Climbing upon the work board supported by two scaffoldings, they were able to set the first piece of wood in place easily. Now, the hard part started. Yanis set the end of the rail at the bow of the boat. Then he asked Billy to hold it firmly, while he drilled two holes completely through the six-inch rail and hull/joint edge of the boat. The holes were spaced about eight inches apart.

"Billy, I'll hold the board now. Could you hand me two long bolts, two washers and two nuts?" Yanis asked. "They're in that box behind you."

Billy turned and found a good size box of stainless hardware. Gathering the fasteners, he turned back toward Yanis.

"Put one in each of the two holes we just drilled," Yanis instructed. "Then take the two washers and nuts, and stick your arm into the anchor locker, here beside me." Yanis lifted the hatch to the anchor locker, exposing a hole in the deck easily large enough for Billy to reach his hand and arm into. "If you can, screw them onto the other end of the bolts we just stuck through our two holes. That will hold the board in place for now."

Billy did as instructed. He tightened the nuts finger tight. Yanis released the new rail.

The rail stuck out at an awkward angle, hanging off the side of the boat because the board was straight, and the boat's hull had a beautiful curve.

"Are you sure that's right?" Billy asked, obviously noticing the disparity between the two.

Without answering, Yanis stepped to the end of the rail and gently pulled it toward the edge of the hull. Billy's question was soon answered as the wooden rail bent ever so slightly, following the curvature of the boat.

"Now," he said, "Billy, take the drill and make another hole through the rail and the hull/deck edge. Measure first with this ruler. Space each hole eight inches apart."

Billy followed his instructions. "I'm through," he said, running the drill bit up and down through his new hole, cleaning out the channel."

"Good, now put another bolt in the hole and secure it below with a washer and nut while I hold the wood," Yanis told him.

After Billy finished, Yanis carefully bent the rail a bit more, easing it toward the edge of the boat by gently pulling on the opposite end. Again, the wooden rail gradually bent into shape.

Billy drilled another hole in the rail eight inches from the last and secured it with another bolt. He then repeated the process until the entire rail was bolted into place.

"Wow," Billy said, admiring how the wooden rail had taken on the flowing shape of the boat's hull. "Would you look at that? It looks like it has always been on this boat. It fits."

"It does look good, doesn't it?" Yanis agreed. "We need to let it sit in this position overnight. The slight bend we have forced the rail into will become natural in time. The wood has a memory. Tomorrow, we will remove the rail, then reinstall it in a bed of sealant and adhesive. Then we'll tighten the bolts down. That process will permanently connect the new caprail to the boat. Then we'll be ready for the next piece." Yanis noticed he was talking as though Billy would be returning the next day to help him again. He hoped he would. He liked Billy.

Yanis stepped down off the scaffolding, walked to his chair and took a seat. Billy followed.

"I appreciate the help, Billy," he continued. "You are welcome here anytime. I can always use your help with one of my boat chores." He motioned Billy toward the other chair. "Okay, where were we with our story?" Yanis asked him.

"You just woke up on the beach under a palm tree," Billy reminded him.

"Oh yes," Yanis said, apparently having made his decision to continue telling Billy his special story. "I remember opening my eyes on the beach. Kneeling beside me was the most attractive young woman I had ever seen. She had the largest brown eyes, long coal black hair and a smile that was absolutely beautiful.

"On my other side an ancient-looking man sat cross-legged. He had a thick gray beard that blended into his long gray hair. Hanging from his left ear was a silver ring about two inches in diameter.

"As you might expect with all that had transpired, I was in a state of shock when I awoke.

"'What has happened?' I asked, alarmed at where I was. 'Where is my sailboat? Who are you? How did I safely get here? The last thing I remember is hitting my head,' I spurted out. Then, I remembered my arm had been badly broken with two bones protruding from a gaping wound. I was scared to look at it, but I had to. I slowly turned my head, expecting the worst." Yanis hesitated a moment to catch his breath, then continued. "My arm was stretched out beside me on the mat. It had no wound. It wasn't mangled. It wasn't torn. It didn't even have a scar. It looked normal. I thought for a moment that I must have been dreaming."

"Really?" Billy stretched his word out in disbelief. "How could that have happened?"

Not giving Billy an answer, the old man continued, "I opened and closed my hand. Everything worked. I looked toward the beautiful young woman. My eyes must have been pleading for an explanation. She reached down and put her hand gently on my forehead.

"'Stay quiet,' she said. 'All is well. Your sailboat is safe. You are safe. We are your friends. I know you have questions. I will try to answer them, one at a time.'

"The young woman's eyes looked so sincere. Her voice was calm and trusting.

"'As far as how you got here, your sailboat brought you. But as far as how you got here safely, that was by the luck of the little yellow bird.

"'Yellow bird?'" I asked bewildered.

"Then she continued to explain. 'After my grandfather, Alexander,' she gestured toward the gray-bearded man sitting by my side, 'saw your sailboat slowly make its way onto the shoal just off the beach, he watched it for a while. Seeing no activity, he waded out to have a look. He found you lying in the cockpit. You were unconscious. Your arm was broken and your head had a nasty bump on it. As he boarded your sailboat to lend assistance, he looked inside the cabin for other people. As he looked down the companionway, the yellow bird flew out.'

"'Yellow bird?' I questioned her again, not understanding its relevance.

"But before she could answer, my focus went back to my arm.

"'What about this?' I continued, motioning to my arm. 'It was broken and split open. How is it not broken, now?'

"'One question at a time,' the young woman answered, 'as far as the yellow bird is concerned, it is common during storms for small birds flying from one island to the next to seek shelter on passing boats. When this happens, if the boat is fortunate enough for the bird to be a Golden Canary, it is believed that safe passage and a prosperous journey will follow. When the Golden Canary flew out from the cabin of your boat, my grandfather knew immediately how someone in your condition could have safely arrived here on the island.'

"'Okay, okay,' I said. 'I do remember the small yellow bird that hopped into my cabin during the storm, but I don't see how it could have had anything to do with my safe arrival. And I don't see how my arm is not broken. I know what it looked like when I passed out.' I continued pleading for more answers. 'This should be impossible,' I said, lifting my fully healed arm up above my head.

"Her answer to my broken arm question was simple. 'My name is Izzy and my grandfather is the Kahuna for our people,' she looked at me as though that answered my question completely.

"'But my arm, how is it no longer broken?' I asked again. 'And what do you mean, your grandfather is the Kahuna for your people?'

"'He is the Kahuna. Actually, he is the last living Kahuna we know of. He is the healer and the teacher for our people,' she reaffirmed. 'He helped you to heal your arm and head. And now if you feel up to it, my grandfather will take you to your sailboat. But I must caution you, I think there is another storm coming. It would be wise for you to stay on the island until it passes.'

"Izzy's answers did nothing more than give me more questions. What had she meant, Alexander helped me heal my arm and head wounds? I questioned her further about it.

"'It would do no good for me to explain further,' she responded. 'You won't understand yet. When the time is right, if you choose further knowledge about this, my grandfather will teach you. But now, just feel the joy of having a healed body. Be thankful for that. You don't always have to know how something happens. When your arm was broken and cut, your obvious desire was for it to be whole again. What is most important is what you want, not how you will get it.'

"I sat up on the mat. 'Of course I'm happy and thankful the wound is healed. It's just that I don't know how it could have happened. Broken body parts don't just heal overnight.'

"'You are correct,' Izzy said. 'In most cases, broken bodies do not heal overnight. But that is not because they can't. It is because you don't think they can. Your mind is full of doubt. Now, before we go further, at least tell me your name.' She tried to change the subject.

"'Yanis, Yanis Barton is my name.' I stated, extending my once-mangled arm in her direction to shake hands.

"'Yanis Barton,' Alexander slowly stated as he unfolded his legs and stood up. 'I will go with you, Yanis Barton, to your sailing vessel. But, as my granddaughter said, you shouldn't head out to sea today. A storm is coming. You may need to stay for several days until it passes. Your sailing vessel is safe in the lagoon. Come, I will take you to her.'

"Alexander leaned down, extending his hand to help me stand. After getting my balance, we started walking in the direction of the point. Izzy stayed behind. As we walked, I lifted and twisted my arm into every position possible. It worked perfectly. I couldn't believe it.

"'You were lucky,' Alexander began. 'The keel to your sailing vessel bumped into the sand on the shoal at the perfect time — dead low tide. The ocean current and wave action was minimal. So she wasn't forced hard aground. I was able to push her back a little and free her from the sand. Then, as the tide came in, I sailed over the shoal into the safety of the lagoon. After anchoring her, I carried you to shore and looked after your wounds.'

"'You say you looked after my wounds. How did you look after them? How did you heal my arm?'

"But, before Alexander could answer, I remembered I hadn't thanked him for his help with my arm or my boat. 'Alexander, let me say this first. I want to thank you for whatever assistance you have given me. I mean, I don't know how you did what you did, but I am grateful for all your help.'

"'Yanis, your gratitude is accepted. And, as far as your healing,' Alexander said, 'I don't think you are ready to hear how your arm was healed. Just be thankful that your arm is whole again.'

"All of the time the old Kahuna was speaking, we were walking across the sand in the direction of the lagoon.

"'I don't know what you mean by not being ready to hear the how. But I am very grateful to you for what you did to heal my arm,' I told him.

"'I didn't heal your arm,' Alexander said.

"'What do you mean by that?' I questioned. 'Look at it.' I held my arm high.

"Alexander smiled at my tenacity; he finally stopped walking and turned toward me.

"'Here is the truth,' he said. 'I didn't heal you. You healed yourself with the Mana Loa you have within. Yes, I did straighten and realign the bones. Then I merely gave your lower self the suggestions it needed to accelerate the healing process. The healing was done by you, from the inside. Not by me.'

"'By me?' I questioned emphatically. 'It's impossible to heal so quickly.'

"'I told you, you weren't ready for the how, Yanis.

Your mind is full of doubt,' the Kahuna said. 'I suggest you think about it this way. Assuming the accident happened on the last day of the storm, which would have been yesterday, if a quick healing were not possible, you would still have a broken and mangled arm. Is that not correct?'

"I thought that statement through for a second and realized he had me. 'Okay,' I furthered, 'let's assume you are correct. Then why wouldn't everyone who is sick heal themselves in the same way? Why would anyone continue being sick or injured?'

"'That is a good question,' Alexander replied. 'However, now is not the right time to begin a lengthy explanation; just believe we all have Mana Loa, an energy flowing through us that if directed properly can bring forth the fulfillment of our deepest desires. It can be directed purposefully or un-purposefully. I merely helped your lower self direct this energy flow toward your desire for a whole and healthy body. It was that simple. Now let's continue. The lagoon is not far and the storm is coming.' Alexander turned and stepped forward. It was obvious to me he didn't care to speak further on the subject.

"I followed closely behind him.

"It was only a few more minutes until we rounded the point and there she sat quietly anchored in a perfectly protected lagoon. I waded out into the water, having to swim the last fifteen or twenty yards before reaching my boat. The lagoon must have been at least ten to twelve feet deep. It was a perfect harbor, safe from tidal changes, even though the tides at that latitude were minimal. It was also safe from ocean swells. They couldn't reach the confines of the lagoon.

"Climbing aboard, I quickly gave my old girl the onceover. I checked all the rigging and lines. The sails were folded properly. The rigging appeared in order. I found nothing broken or out of place. She had survived the storm very well.

"*She must have done it,* I thought. *This old girl must have sailed me here, by herself. But how did she do it? And where was here? That's right, I remember. Izzy never said where we were.* I turned expecting Alexander to be right there with me, but he wasn't. Looking toward the beach, I saw him walking back to the point.

"I sat down in the cockpit. Leaning back, I closed my eyes and tried to remember all that had transpired. *How did I really get here? I know what they said about the yellow bird, but come on now. That was hard to believe. And how did my arm get healed, really? I mean, I know what Alexander said. But how did it really heal? And where am I?* As I lay there pondering these questions, I marveled at the clear sunny sky. To me, it sure didn't look like a storm was coming. The weather looked beautiful. I lay there for a while and drifted off to sleep.

"Knock, Knock, Knock! The sound of someone knocking on the side of the boat woke me abruptly. As I opened my eyes, I saw Izzy pulling herself up and over the side of the sailboat.

"'My grandfather thought I should come out and check on you,' she said. 'You have been out here for a couple of hours. The storm is coming quickly.'

"Remembering the crystal clear sunny skies, I looked up. The sky had now taken on a different complexion. Dark clouds had in fact moved in and looked menacing.

"'My grandfather wondered if you were going to wait out the storm here on your boat, or would you like to come to our hut and wait it out there?' Izzy asked.

"'Where is your hut?' I questioned.

"'It is inland from where you awoke on the beach.' She gestured toward the high mountain. 'The higher elevations offer better protection in stormy conditions. My grandfather feels this will be a very bad storm. You would be safer inland.'

"The weather did seem to be getting worse and worse by the minute. And after surviving the storm a few days before, somehow the sound of a few more days ashore seemed inviting.

"'Is there room in the hut for all three of us,' I questioned further.

"'There is plenty of room,' she replied.

"'I would like to come ashore if it is no inconvenience,' I told her. 'Let me get some clean clothes. Before we go I need to make sure everything is secure here.'

"'Good,' she said. 'Hurry. The rain is already starting.'

"Within a couple of minutes, we were on our way. I had to swim half the distance to shore, holding my bag of clothes up in the air with one hand while paddling with the other. Once ashore, it started raining much harder. The clothes I held above my head during the swim were now drenched from rainwater. Izzy and I both laughed at my failed attempt to keep them dry. Turning, I ran behind Izzy down the beach.

"When we finally reached the spot where I lay on the mat earlier, the mat was gone.

"'Alexander is at the hut,' Izzy said. 'It's this way.'

"It wasn't long before we reached the base of the mountain where Alexander's hut was perched. We turned inland and the terrain became much steeper. We were down to just a steady walk on the steep incline. The jungle foliage was thick on either side of the trail. We walked as quickly as we could, but we still made slow progress.

"Finally, we broke out of the thickest part of the jungle and entered a beautiful open, grassy meadow. On the far side of the meadow sat a small hut made from split trees. Palm fronds covered its roof and were secured with a light rope. The front porch was also covered by a palm frond roof. Alexander waved at us as we entered the meadow.

"'I'm glad you two made it up here when you did,' he said, pointing back behind us. Turning, I saw a view that was absolutely breathtaking. From that vantage point I could see for miles and miles down the jungle-covered mountain and far out to sea. I could also see giant black thunderheads moving in our direction. The heavier rain was quickly working its way up the mountainside. It was just minutes behind us. From that vantage point, I could even see the lagoon where my sailboat sat safely moored.

"As we stepped up onto the porch, I commented to Alexander, 'This is quite a place you have. Did you build it?'

"'Yes, in a way I did,' he retorted with a chuckle. 'I knew in my mind precisely what I wanted. The rest was easy.'

"Here we go again, I thought. *Another Alexander riddle I wouldn't understand.*

"'There are towels inside. Put on some dry clothes,' he continued. 'Yanis, I have some pants and shirts lying on my bed. Try them on and see if they fit. Even if they don't, they'll be better than the wet ones.'

"'Beggars can't be choosers,' I responded, entering the hut.

"The storm blew in and it rained for three days. We sat inside Alexander's hut telling stories about our lives while getting further acquainted. I really liked these people, Billy, especially Izzy."

Yanis stood from his chair and stretched. He had been telling his story to Billy for over two hours. Slowly he slid his chair over to the wall and sat back down.

Billy thought he knew what that meant: nap time.

But instead, almost on cue, in came Elizabeth. "Lunch time, you two," she said. "I've got sandwiches and juice."

She walked over to a small table sitting next to the two chairs. "How is the boat work coming and, of course, the stories?" she asked.

"Well," Billy said. "Mr. Barton has been telling me about waking up after a fierce storm only to find himself on a beautiful island with an old Kahuna named Alexander and his beautiful granddaughter with long coal-black hair. Her name was Izzy. It appears the Kahuna miraculously helped Mr. Barton heal his broken arm. He broke it in a boat accident during a storm, and…" At this point, Billy stopped. "Mrs. Barton, you've probably heard this story plenty of times."

"You are right, Billy, I know the story by heart," she confirmed, smiling affectionately.

"Let's eat," Yanis said. "I'm starving. Then after lunch, I need to go into town and see my painter. I need to get on his work schedule. He's usually booked weeks in advance. I want him to come paint this boat as soon as the rails are on. Maybe we can continue the story tomorrow, Billy. I could use your help again, if you have the time. Do you think you can come by?"

"You bet I can," Billy said with excitement, wolfing down his sandwich. He was hungrier than he realized. Between the boat work and the stories, he had temporarily forgotten about the sales agreement he had in his briefcase. With renewed excitement, he remembered he needed to turn it in at the office. He couldn't wait to tell his manager about his success. More importantly, he wanted to call Dana. *She would be so excited,* he thought. This had truly been another big day for Billy McCoy.

Yanis smiled at Billy's agreement to return the following day.

All the while Elizabeth just sat there slowly eating her sandwich, watching her husband. *A beautiful young woman with coal-black hair,* she thought, remembering Billy's description. *The old man was really telling the story. This is good.* She was happy.

5

THE PATHWAY

When dreams are seen through eyes of doubt
Their seeds will die away,
They cannot grow when seen without
Expectancy and faith.

O n the drive back into town, Billy realized he was
feeling anxious. He thought about the comments
and praise his manager would surely give him. He
imagined seeing his name high up the leader board, surely
at the top. Nobody else had ever turned in over fifteen sales
contracts in one day; at least, nobody Billy knew about.
There was something about the attention he expected to get
that made him anxious. Even though Billy's dream had always been to climb to the top of the leader board, now that it
was happening he was feeling a little bit uncertain.

In some ways, Billy felt this good fortune should
be shared only between him and Dana. He knew he would
have to tell his manager about it because every morning his
manager reviewed the prior day's production sheets. If Billy
turned in the large contract that day or the next, his manager

would see the numbers anyway. His name would be put in first position on the sales board and he would have to deal with the attention of his fellow sales associates. This made Billy anxious. He was unsure whether he would like being in the spotlight or not.

Billy's decision about what to do was made for him. The first person he encountered in the office was his manager. "How's it going today, Billy?" he asked.

"Fantastic, thank you," Billy replied.

"How'd you do with the leads I shared with you a couple days ago?" his manager asked. "I noticed you turned in a couple sales contracts earlier this morning. Was that from the leads?"

"Yes, two of the leads you shared with me purchased last night," Billy confirmed. "They also gave me a few referrals."

"Were you able to make contact with Yanis Barton? I'm curious about that one. You know, ever since his name turned up the other day, he has come up several times in conversation. It appears Mr. Barton is quite an extraordinary person. His charitable giving statewide is remarkable. And I hear his wife is just the same."

Caught unprepared, Billy realized he had no choice but to be truthful with his manager.

Shuffling his feet, he took a stance and replied. "Mr. and Mrs. Barton are the most caring, giving and friendly people I think I have ever met. Having only known them for two days I can tell you without a doubt they are both very extraordinary."

"And, what about the lead card with Yanis' name on it?" his manager questioned. "Did Yanis Barton actually send it in?"

"Yes, he did," Billy said. "He wanted information about the product. He loved the idea. His wife knows a lady who owns one and she raves about it. So it was only natural for the Barton's to buy one."

"Well, that's great! It's even more than great," his manager exclaimed with excitement! "It has already been a very productive week for you. I am so happy for you, Billy. I knew this career would turn around for you. I just knew it. Hard work, you know? What about referrals from the Bartons? Referrals are the lifeblood of our business, you know that? They have quite a few people working on their farm. I bet that could be a good source of future business for you."

"Well, no that wouldn't be," Billy replied quickly.

"Oh and why's that?" his manager asked, not understanding Billy's response.

"Well," Billy said, "Mr. and Mrs. Barton have already purchased one for each of their employees."

"Really," his manager replied. "When did they do that?"

"Just this morning," Billy told him as he reached into his briefcase and pulled out the purchase agreement. "Here's the order."

His manager took the purchase agreement and began to look it over. At first, he didn't say a word. Then his eyes scanned down the quantity column.

"Wow," is all he could muster as he looked at it for

the second and third time.

"Fifteen, they really bought fifteen?" his manager said loudly, looking at Billy for confirmation.

"Yes they did," Billy confirmed, handing his manager their check. They bought one for themselves, and fourteen for their employees."

"I have never had a salesperson turn in an order of this size in one day," his manager said. "As a matter of fact, I have never had a salesperson turn in this many sales in an entire week. You do know what this is going to do to the sales board, Billy? You will easily take over first position. Even those who are regularly on top will be blown away and we're only a few days into the month."

The sales production board was a big thing to Billy's manager. He felt it added a bit of healthy competition between the salespeople. He felt it was a positive stimulation.

"I know what it will do," Billy said, bashfully. "Maybe we should hold off putting them up on the board. Or maybe we should put them up gradually throughout the rest of the month?"

"Absolutely not," his manager objected forcefully. "This is something you should be proud of, son. This is your business, Billy. This is the business of every person involved in this office. If it were not for you folks, the salespeople, out there selling our product, none of the rest of us would have jobs. There would be no office. And this level of production, Billy, is something you should be very proud of. It is something others will respect you for. Every industry has salespeople. Without their success, the industry fails. It is just that simple."

Billy understood his manager's emotional outburst, but that didn't lesson his embarrassment from all the attention he knew was coming. Billy knew his manager was correct. After all, Billy was a salesperson. This was his occupation. He should be proud of it. But salesman or not, Billy still had reservations.

As he left his manager's office, Billy questioned what had really transpired. He hadn't gotten all the orders through his salesmanship. It was Mr. Barton's idea to make the purchase in the first place. And as far as the additional orders, they were certainly not from Billy's efforts or suggestions. It was Mr. Barton's suggestion and Mrs. Barton's agreement. It's more like the sale fell out of the air. It's not like Billy gave an awe-inspiring presentation to fifteen people.

Even though Billy was totally elated with his success over the past couple of days, he was also bewildered. He was confused with how to repeat it. Being in the right place at the right time seemed to be the only explanation to Billy. But in his mind there had to be another reason. It couldn't just be fate or happenchance. Like Mr. Barton said that morning, "You had a product and I had a desire." *But, what brought my product and his desire together?* Billy wondered. *If I could ever figure out the answer to that question, my sales career would explode.*

Billy quickly finished at the office and left for home. He wanted to call Dana in privacy. That would be a special call. He didn't want to make it from the office.

"Are you sitting down?" Billy asked Dana, trying to

contain his excitement.

"Why?" she responded, not actually sitting. "What's up?"

"I just thought you might like to know," he hesitated for a moment, "I turned in seventeen purchase orders today." Billy finished his statement and quietly awaited her response.

"Are you kidding me?" Dana questioned, stunned at his statement. "Seventeen orders? Billy, that's over twice as many as you sold in the last six months. You're kidding, aren't you? If you're not, I do have to sit down."

"You'd better sit down then," Billy confirmed. "I'm not kidding. I think I finally got the break I've been looking for. Hopefully, it won't be long and you guys will be homeward bound." His excitement was showing now. He couldn't wait to have his family home.

"I'm so proud of you, Honey," Dana told him. "How did you ever sell so many in such a short period of time? We've only been gone two days. We should have left a long time ago."

Billy smiled at her comment. "Well, I guess I don't know the real reason. I'm trying to figure that out. I've been thinking about it most of the afternoon. All I do know is my manager gave me some leads yesterday. And one of those leads happened to be a man and his wife who own a huge farm just outside of town. When I went out for the presentation, they were so impressed they decided to place an order for all their employees. They have fourteen people employed at their farm. And then they wanted one for themselves. The other two sales I made were last evening's two appointments.

"Even that, Billy, you have never made two sales in one evening," Dana quickly interjected. "How did that happen?"

"Again, Dana, I don't know for sure. I'm still kind of in shock myself over all this. Dana, these people are the nicest people I think I've ever met. I almost feel like I took advantage of them. I mean, I know I didn't, but I kind of feel guilty about how easily this all came together. I feel like I need to talk with them again and make sure they really want to do this. I know how badly we need the income, but..." Billy's voice trailed away.

Dana could tell he was struggling. "Maybe you should, Billy, before we get our hopes up about the income. Maybe you should talk with them again," Dana encouraged. "If you don't this may continue to bother you. But if you do talk to them and they still feel positive about their decision, then you need to feel positive about it, too."

"Yes, I think you're right," Billy said. "I think I'll go out there this afternoon," he continued, glancing at his watch to make sure it wasn't too late.

He told Dana he'd call her later. He hung up the phone and immediately left for the Barton farm. It was only four o'clock.

Goose stood up and slowly stretched while she waited for the approaching car to get close enough to hear her bark. One woof was all she let out before recognizing Billy's car as it pulled up.

Yanis and Elizabeth sat in the swing on the front porch almost every afternoon. That day was no exception. They both waved at Billy as he got out of the car.

"Here comes our wayward salesman," Yanis affectionately said to Elizabeth.

"I wonder if he forgot something."

"I don't think so," Yanis returned.

"I hope you don't mind me coming back for a few minutes," he said, stepping up on the front porch. "I just needed to speak with you folks about something."

"Not at all," Elizabeth told him. "We love having you come by. Come anytime. We've told you that."

"Well," Billy spoke now on a more serious note. "You guys have been so kind to me. I just wanted to make sure you were still happy with your purchase. I need to know you are still comfortable with the decision you made."

"Why, I think it was a wonderful decision," Yanis spoke out quickly. "Why would I have made the purchase if I didn't? I can't wait until the delivery date."

Billy silently let out a sigh of relief. "I'm so glad to hear you say that; I just needed to make sure," Billy returned. "This sale means a lot to my family and me. When I got to the office today, my manager made such a huge deal out of the size of the order. He made it sound so out of the ordinary that I kind of felt guilty about it.

"After leaving the office, I called my wife, Dana. We spoke, not just about the size of the order, but about the way I was feeling. I just felt a bit uncomfortable. I decided it would be best if I came back to the farm to make sure you folks still felt content and happy with your decision. I don't want to feel like I took advantage of you in any way. I've come to respect you both very much, in a very short period of time. And I love coming out working on the old boat and, of course, hearing the stories, real or not." His eyes glanced toward Yanis prankishly. Both Yanis and Elizabeth laughed at his comment.

Billy really did wonder if Yanis was telling him some tall-tale of the sea or the truth. But either way, Billy didn't care; he just loved listening to the old man talk.

"And, there's something else," Billy continued quickly before they could respond. "I wasn't completely forthright earlier today when you asked me about my family. It is true they have gone to visit Dana's parents. But not just for a visit. They actually moved back for a while. Possibly up to ninety days. They just left a couple of days ago. My sales career has not been very successful to this point. I haven't made fifteen sales in the full six months I've been employed by the company. My manager says this is sometimes normal. He says it often takes a year or more to really get going in the business. But when we started we didn't have a year's worth of savings set aside for support, we had only enough for six months. When that ran out, we were forced into a decision. We agreed that if in ninety days I have not reached the sales goals Dana and I decided upon, I would quit the sales business and move home to her and the kids. However, if I do reach our agreed-upon sales goal, she and the kids would move back to Colorado and I would continue my career in the sales industry. This life in Colorado is what we both dream of.

"Your order today gave me a much-needed boost. It is a jump-start to my career, you might say. And I just wanted you both to know how much my family and I appreciate it. That's all." Billy felt himself getting emotional again so he said no more.

Yanis stood, glancing down at Elizabeth. He knew she had quickly grown as attached to Billy as he had. He felt Billy's sincerity that was being demonstrated. *With the proper guidance and knowledge, this young man could do very well in a sales career or any other life pursuit,* Yanis thought.

Elizabeth caught Yanis' glance and slightly nodded. "Billy's Kaula-O is strong," she replied softly. They loved to meet people who showed noteworthy signs of consideration toward others. It was one of the characteristics they most admired. Consideration for all life, complete honesty with yourself and others, and your ability to recognize and act on your deepest feelings, these were the ingredients they called 'Kaula-O.' This signifies that his passageway from emotion to action was clear. Dreams could be fulfilled quickly.

Yanis now looked down at Billy. "I have something important to say and it's something I truly hope you understand."

Yanis shifted slightly, getting ready to deliver his point. "You cannot and will not ever receive anything in your life unless it is what you expect to receive, on the inside. The only way you can receive something is if you have created a pathway for it, a pathway allowing it to come to you.

"In this case, I had the simple need to find a gift for all my employees. Out of curiosity I returned your card and, look, it turned out to be exactly what we were looking for." Yanis said. "And we got a bonus. I didn't know it would bring such a truly caring friend as you, Billy. I want you to know how much we appreciate your honesty. But," he held his hand up to signify something else of importance, "what I do know is this: I always get what I expect because I always expect situations in my life such as this, a perfect win-win experience. We both got what we wanted and we both are very happy with the outcome. Correct?" Yanis waited for Billy's reply.

"Yes, Sir, that is correct," Billy said, still trying to fully understand Yanis' statement, but not completely grasping its magnitude.

"But, what makes that happen? Billy asked. "I have worked for six months now, trying to make an income my family could live on. I fully expected to succeed at this sales career from the very beginning, that's why I came here and took the job in the first place."

Yanis sat back down on the swing next to Elizabeth while Billy explained, "In six months, I have made very few sales. Then in a matter of just a few days, and of course," Billy added cynically, "just after I sent my family back home to live with her folks and we endured all the 'I told you so' comments, I begin to make some sales. The timing with this whole thing kind of makes me angry.

"Why couldn't this bit of success have come a few days ago? Sending my family back was such an embarrassing thing to do. Failure has been the single-largest concern I have had to live with for the last six months. After all the work I put in, I still failed to make enough money for us to live on. I had no other choice but to send my family home. It's almost like it was preplanned or predestined or something. I've been thinking about this all afternoon. To me, it appears the only answer for my current success is that I was in the right place at the right time. That's all there is to it. But I know there has to be another reason. If only I could figure that one out, my career would really be on its way."

"Billy, young man, without realizing it, I think you might have answered your own question. If what you say is true, then it's possible your sluggish sales and your family separation was preplanned, not predestined," Yanis told him. "There is a difference. I'll explain that difference in a few minutes. But first, let me say this. If you feel fear of failing every day, especially when your family really needs the income, the emotion behind the feeling will magnify, dominating your thoughts.

"The emotion behind the thought is sent out into the creative world to attract back to you situations and events that mimic its vibration. That means if what you feel every day is anxiety and tension based on a desperate need to make sales, and you give yourself six months to fail or succeed, then failure is pretty much the only possibility for you.

"It sounds to me like you have preplanned the situation you find yourself in since the day you came to Colorado. This fear of failing has been working constantly to open and maintain a perfect pathway for it to happen. Your fears return to you daily as unsuccessful sales appointments, tension in the family and, of course, more fear-based thoughts that will continue to attract in their likeness. Billy, you accomplished what you expected without realizing what you were doing. The emotion from your fear feelings attracted back to you in their likeness.

"Over the last six months, you created your current situation according to the thought you allowed to be dominant in your mind. The thought was backed with powerful feelings fueled by inner emotions of fear. It is exactly as Alexander taught. Fear, guilt, anger, hatred all fill your thoughts with negative emotions that block your pathway to prosperity and success." Here Yanis hesitated a moment.

"This emotional vibration you speak of, Mr. Barton," Billy replied, "where does it come from?"

"Your thoughts and emotions are vibrations of energy," Yanis answered. "If you think thoughts predominately of a negative vibration, then those thought vibrations go forth only to attract back to you situations or life experiences in their likeness. But if you think thoughts of a positive vibration such as love, joy, success, appreciation, etc., these will also return to you as situations you desire, like great success, great relationships, health, etc.

"It appears to me that over the last six months you have preplanned your current situation with thoughts based predominately on a negative emotion. By not directing your thinking process, you allowed negative emotions to surface and fuel your thoughts with feelings of fear, thereby preplanning what has taken place. Here we can see the difference between preplanning and predestination. Predestination suggests that a person has no other option. What will happen will happen and you haven't the power to change it, while a preplanned life is one in which you are the director.

"Positive vibrations sent forth in thought will mirror back to you as a positive experience. Think truly positive thoughts of success backed with feelings charged with positive emotion and you will attract success into your life. The emotion behind the thought is the key.

"Billy, it absolutely cannot and will not be any other way. If success in business is what you desire, put forth great appreciation for the sales you make and success will continue to flow to you. Appreciation is one of the most powerful emotions you have. You are a magnet attracting success into your life from all angles. You must remember this point. If you allow your mind to stay focused on the dollars needed for rent, food, clothing, etc., and back those thoughts with feelings of fear and scarcity, all you will attract into your life are more situations based on fear and scarcity. This is a 'not enough' attitude. And not enough is what you will get.

"You must always focus and think on success, even when sales appear to be slow on the outside. That is when it's the most critical not to let the focus move back to scarcity. Instead, be tenacious and keep the focus on your performance goals, number of sales, number of appointments, prospective phone calls, advertisement avenues, etc. Keep your mind off the dollars and stay focused on the action steps necessary for high-performance sales.

"Back your thoughts with the actions of a successful salesperson, by doing what other successful salespeople do. Stay focused on your intention, which is not becoming successful, but instead is continuing to be successful. Don't place your success somewhere out there; know and feel your success right now. As you hold this intention clearly in your mind, you will recognize small things in your life change in your favor. When you do, be grateful for the changes because you are creating the pathway through which your dreams are fulfilled. As you empower your life and embrace this positive attitude, the success you dreamed of yesterday will unfold as the achievements you enjoy today. And Billy, you will not always know from what direction the success will come. As you grow in your expectancy of greater success and higher achievements, more and more dollars will flow to you according to your needs and desires.

"You see, Billy, your success creates your wealth; wealth can never create success. You must create your wealth by becoming successful in your mind. Alexander says, 'to have on the outside, you first must be on the inside.'"

Billy sat quietly for a moment. Though Yanis' explanation was lengthy, Billy felt he was beginning to understand what the old man was saying. But he had questions.

"Mr. Barton," Billy said, "how long does it take your thoughts to have an effect on your life? And what is the difference between your thoughts, your feelings and your emotions?"

"Those are good questions, Billy. Let me answer the second question first. Alexander taught that first you have a thought. And from that thought a belief held in your lower self, Unihipili, produces an emotion, Mana Loa. The emotion, whether it's love or fear, fuels the feeling, a sensation in your entire body that is felt by your conscious mind, Uhane. The vibration of that feeling partners immediately with your thought. The picture of your thought is sent forth into the creative world at the vibration level of the feeling you felt.

"The unusual names that Alexander used for our subconscious mind, conscious mind or emotion is not the important thing here. What is important is the directing of our thoughts and emotions to create the desired outcome.

"Now, whether the vibration sent out is positive or negative depends upon the emotion created by the subconscious mind or your lower self when you first have the thought. You see, certain thoughts trigger certain emotions held deep inside you. Some will be negative and some will be positive. If you wish to direct your life in accordance with your desired dreams, you must learn to use the thinking process wisely to produce only positive emotions. They are the fuel of positive thoughts. Do you understand?"

"I think I do," Billy responded. "If I let my mind think even for a second about ninety days without my family, I feel sadness and my stomach knots up from the negative emotion. However, if I think about my recent sales success and its benefits, I immediately feel gratitude and great joy."

"That is exactly right," Yanis confirmed, amazed at how quickly Billy was catching on. "Now, your other question was, how long does it take a thought to create. It depends on the thought. Your fear of having to send your family home manifested precisely as you planned. You knew you had six months worth of saved income and your fear was associated with running short of money due to insufficient sales. So you created what you feared, being out of money in six months.

"Alexander taught the actual energy within a thought is dependent upon the amount and intensity of the emotion that is fueling it. If you think a thought clearly and back it with powerful emotion, creation can be very quick."

Billy started to take the information Yanis gave him and apply it to his life. *The more I think about my situation, the more I realize my most dominate feeling over this past six months has been fear of not being successful.* Billy thought to himself. *Sure, I talked success and may have tried to act confident, but all the while deep down inside, I see now I actually feared failing more than I ever expected success. I just didn't realize it at the time.*

"I do understand what you're saying, but how could things change so dramatically, almost overnight?" Billy asked. "For six months I continuously struggled to make sales, then over a short couple of days I have received success greater than the entire prior six months. How does that happen?"

"Simple," Yanis suggested. "For six months you preplanned your negative results with constant negative emotions of fear of failing. Once your family left, you might say the finale to your preplanning took place. Now, it's like a new slate. You obviously have not been obsessed with more thoughts of failing. Otherwise, your sales would not have increased the way they have. I believe acceptance to your family's situation released a certain pressure you had on yourself. You now have only been thinking about getting your family back. You have been focused on what it will take to make that happen. Your desire to succeed has been here all along. It just has not been given the proper fuel through positive thoughts and expectancy, until now."

Yanis continued to hold Billy's attention. "I don't want to change the subject or anything, but you said something earlier I haven't had an opportunity to respond to. Your comment, 'as far as my tall-tales, whether true or not,' remember?"

Billy let out a nervous laugh. "I remember," he said. "I was just kidding."

The old man smiled and continued. "Do you remember me saying earlier there were two things that happened in my sailing story that changed my life forever?"

"Yes, I remember," Billy responded.

Here, Yanis stood again and made a big deal about reaching toward his wife and taking her hand. He helped her stand. "Here is the first and most important thing that changed my life. Izzy Barton, I would like to introduce you to Billy McCoy."

Izzy Barton, Billy thought, smiling at the old man. *What did he mean, Izzy? This was Elizabeth. Izzy was in his story.* A look of surprise slipped across Billy's face as he looked into Elizabeth's big beautiful brown eyes. *Her long brown hair has turned silver.* Billy shook his head with bewilderment.

The old couple started laughing aloud, knowing Billy figured it out.

Billy stepped forward and Izzy embraced him. "You are so special," she whispered in his ear. "As Alexander would say, you are strong with Kaula-O."

"Mrs. Barton," Billy said, stepping back slowly. "You have referred to this Kaula-O several times now. I'm not sure what you mean. I know of nothing that I have that others do not."

"You are correct, Billy. What I refer to is your awareness of your feelings. It's not that you possess something others do not. Everybody has feelings and everybody feels their feelings. But you have a heightened awareness of yours. And when you feel them, you act on them.

"Unfortunately, most people don't acknowledge their feelings to themselves or to others. This is not done purposely, it's done out of habit. They don't realize the value their feelings provide. Not only can your feelings be a kind of guidance system, but as you can see, they play a vital role in the creation of your life experiences. Instead of directing emotion-packed feelings to partner with and empower your thoughts, which in return create and fulfill your dreams, many allow their lives to go undirected, very similar to your last six months. But," Izzy said with emphasis, "if directed properly, the awareness you have of your feelings can be utilized to great advantage.

"You can purposefully send forth powerful thoughts of desire backed with positive emotion. If you stay focused on them, they will be fulfilled. Alexander said the clear pathway between the lower self and the higher self was Kaula-O. He taught that Mana Loa or energy is transferred through this pathway. It was his belief that energy sent forth in the form of emotions is necessary to fulfill one's desires. And Billy, utilization of this knowledge can be your free ticket to life's 'Prosperity Train.'"

"This is all new information to me," Billy said, shaking his head, a little confused. "You said feelings can be a guidance system and can be used to create your life's experiences. Though," Billy continued, slowly thinking before he spoke, "I must admit, I may be the perfect example of what you are saying. There is no question that over the last six months, my dominate thought was fear of failing. If I was sending negative vibrations out to attract back to me in their likeness, success would have been impossible. I see now how I was preplanning failure all the while."

"Yes, that is it," Yanis said. "Your thoughts have preplanned your life. And as far as the guidance system, let me give you an example.

"Billy, you said you went to your office today to turn in your purchase contracts. There was a big deal made by the office manager in reference to the size of your order. This attention made you uncomfortable. Rather than ignoring those feelings, suppressing them and letting them go undirected, you left the office and spoke to your wife about them. Then, you acted on them and came to our farm. You have a heightened awareness of your feelings and the emotions that fuel them. This awareness creates a clear pathway to your dreams. In Alexander's way of thinking, Kaula-O was simply the clear connection between your lower self and your higher self."

"I think I understand what you are saying. I am very aware of the emotions that create my feelings. Though, I have never looked at them as a guidance system."

"Well, look at it this way," Yanis said, "when you recognized your feelings today, you acted on them by coming to the farm. You spoke with us and realized that all was well. Now, any feelings you have associated with the order we made today will have a positive vibration attached to it — a success vibration. Do you see that?"

"Yes," Billy replied.

"But," Yanis furthered, "had you not come out to the farm, and instead held onto those anxious feelings of uncertainty, never knowing how we really felt, you would feel fearful again, a negative emotion. What vibration do you think that negative emotion would send out?"

"It would probably be negative and attract more failure," responded Billy.

"Correct," Yanis confirmed.

"Come sit at the kitchen table while I prepare dinner," Izzy said. "Billy, you are staying for dinner, aren't you?"

"Oh, I don't want to impose," he responded. "I'm taking up way too much of your time."

"Nonsense," she objected. "What do you think two old folks like us would be doing if we weren't talking to you? There is nothing we enjoy more than having friends visit. So it's settled. Come on in."

"Who you calling old?" Yanis interjected.

Izzy smiled at him.

Billy hesitantly stepped inside the Barton's home. He

really didn't want to be a pest, but he was very interested in what they were teaching him.

"I would like to hear more about what the old Kahuna taught," Billy said as he sat down at the table with Yanis. "It sounds almost, well, for lack of a better word, *magical*."

"Alexander taught us the lessons of the old Kahuna masters. He didn't describe his way of life in words such as 'thoughts being energy vibrations.' Phrases like that come from our years of taking Alexander's teachings and expanding them with the knowledge we have learned on our own. His teachings were of ancient descent and passed down using symbols and many coded words. It was his teachings that Izzy and I built our lives around. It has only been recently we have learned an explanation of his teachings using modern physics and more familiar terms."

"How were his teachings different?" asked Billy.

"Well to explain that, it might be easier if we continue the story we started this morning. If I recall," Yanis said, "we left off where I was sitting with Izzy and Alexander in the hut. I questioned Alexander about the healing of my mangled arm. For three days he avoided my questions and always moved to another subject."

Yanis paused for a moment and looked at his wife, wanting to include her in the story. "If I recollect, Izzy, the storm was just ending. We all stepped out onto the front porch for some fresh air. I sat down on the edge of the porch, looking out at the ocean, far below. I remember thinking how endless the sky appeared. That's when Alexander simply said. 'It was your Kaula-O, Yanis. It was the transfer of your Mana Loa that healed your arm.'

"'Mana Loa?' I questioned Alexander.

"'Yes,' he confirmed, fully understanding that I didn't know what he meant. 'Mana Loa moves through you, empowering you to create your life experiences.'"

Izzy stood at the counter making dinner, while keeping tabs on the story Yanis was telling. She was ready to remind him of anything, if necessary. It amazed her just how excited Yanis got the few times he told this story, especially when he spoke about Alexander.

"Billy," Yanis said, "Alexander talked in words and symbols I was unfamiliar with. It was hard for me to follow his teachings because he used the ancient dialect passed down from one Kahuna to the next. These teachings were shared only between a Kahuna and their initiates. In the past, this information was not shared with everyone. The teachings were held in complete secrecy. This was how Alexander learned the teachings, from the previous Kahuna. You see, Billy, in old world Polynesian dialects the word *Huna* means 'the secret.' The word *Kahuna* means, 'keeper of the secret.' What we are teaching you is part of the secret they held so private among so few.

"The secret was that any desire can be achieved if a person did only three things. They must plant the seed of the desire, have complete faith the seed will grow and accept its fulfillment into their life. That's it. Of course, the old Kahunas had a certain process they utilized to accomplish these steps."

Yanis noticed that Billy was leaning toward him, still

intently focused on what he was saying.

"They taught a process very similar to what we have discussed this evening, except they used different words, such as *Mana Loa, Unihipili, Uhane* and *Aumakua*. But we won't use the ancient dialect. It is much too difficult to memorize a new vocabulary while learning new concepts at the same time.

"The old Kahunas believed the creation process was found in three simple steps. However, one of their secrets was that the first step had two essential parts. First, you planted the seed of your dream in the garden of your mind by clearly imagining the dream as already accomplished. The second part of the first step is empowering the dream seed with the emotion of joy of success, which comes naturally when you see your dream already completed. They sit for a moment breathing deeply to fuel the emotion they release. These two parts in the first step are essential. They present a very clear picture of exactly what is desired and at the same time back the desire with positive joyful emotion. This fuels the return of their desire.

"Now, the second step is found in the Kahuna's strong belief and faith in the process. It is the knowing without a doubt that the fulfillment of the desire is inevitable. In their mind, it was created at some level the second they imagined it. But, until you have gained this confidence in the process, you must visualize this emotionally charged dream over and over again until your Unihipili or lower self is willing to accept it as possible. This allows for the third step.

"The third step is your willingness to accept or allow

this dream fulfillment into your life. The Kahuna believe the easiest way to do this is through gratitude of accomplishment. Gratitude is a powerful emotion, Billy. The old world masters taught that it was important to sit quietly each day, for just a few minutes, working on your desires by using your imagination and powerfully charged thoughts. The complete expectancy of success and lack of doubt opens the natural pathway from your lower and higher self. Your acceptance allows the fulfillment of your dreams to materialize in the physical."

"What type of dreams did Alexander have?" Billy asked. "Did he dream of having lots of money, you know, some type of great success?"

Izzy turned toward the table and said. "Well, to my grandfather, success wasn't having lots of money," she responded. "Success to Alexander was found in feeling great fulfillment in his life. Over sixty years ago, the need for money on our island was not important. We were far more concerned with a good catch of fish or a bountiful harvest of fruit. We seldom even bought food because our islands provided, much like Barton Farms provides most of our needs today.

"Alexander was very clear when he described success. He enjoyed discussing what he called one's journey up 'Dream Mountain.' He asked us what we expected to find when we reached the top of 'Dream Mountain.' Our first answer was obvious: success of reaching the top, of course. He would always laugh thinking that was so funny. 'No,' he would say. 'At the top of Dream Mountain you will find another mountain. That is what life is all about. Changing and growing through the challenge of getting to the top. Each mountain you climb reveals another higher mountain in the distance to challenge you further. And here is the secret you learn as you climb Dream Mountain. The success you seek is found in the journey up the mountain. It becomes your state of mind because with the accomplishment of each challenge your expectancy of further achievement becomes habit. You soon realize you are the success you once sought to be." Izzy paused here for a moment. Then she continued, "Here's the next question."

"And what might that be?" Yanis asked.

"Are you boys ready to eat? Because dinner is served," she said. "Billy, I think we have given you a lot to think about in a short period of time. Don't be concerned with understanding and remembering all of Alexander's old-world teachings. Though his principles still work, we now know the reasons why. And it is no longer a secret. This information is for anyone who is willing to seek it out."

Billy smiled at the caring woman. He shook his head, amazed he had met her. She sat down and they enjoyed their meal, together.

"Mrs. Barton," Billy said. "I have a question. This process you are sharing with me works on any desire, correct?"

"Yes, it applies to any desire you have," Izzy replied.

He smiled. "Wow, what an opportunity."

"Billy," Yanis said. "I think I hear that 'Prosperity

Train' a coming."

The 'Prosperity Train' they keep talking about, Billy thought, smiling, *I kind of like the sound of that.*

Before he left, Yanis asked Billy if he could come and help him with the boat the following day.

"Of course I will be back tomorrow," he said, walking out the front door. "I already have a ticket on the train."

They all laughed at his humor.

Billy thanked the Barton's for all that transpired that day before heading back to town. He had lots to think about.

That night Billy told his wife all about the teachings the Barton's shared. Though the ideas were new and seemed foreign, he wasn't opposed to their possibility. The Barton's success and kindness was validation enough.

That night, he lay in bed thinking about what desire he had that was most important. He knew immediately. He closed his eyes and imagined his kids jumping on his bed with his wife lying beside him. He fell asleep quickly feeling the thrill and joy of their presence. He knew it had been another good, good day.

6

EXPECTANCY

Feelings power thoughts to create
Only in their likeness,
Think not of fear or guilt or hate
Think only joy and kindness.

When Billy got up the next morning, he was quick to get ready and head to the office. Even though his manager thought he should be proud to have zoomed to the top of the sales leader board, Billy was still a bit uncomfortable. So he wanted to get to the office and finish his business before the other salespeople arrived. All he needed at the office was paperwork for the two appointments he had scheduled for that evening. He'd been able to reach two of the referrals shared with him the night before last. Each sounded positive and wanted to hear Billy's presentation.

When Billy arrived at the office, no one was there. He made his way into the large sales room where the sales board hung on the wall.

He looked at the board. There it was, Billy McCoy, at

the very top. He was eleven sales ahead of the nearest sales-person for the month.

As Billy looked at the board, his feelings started to change. Anxiety wasn't dominating his feelings now, as he had expected. Instead, he felt a certain sense of pride in his accomplishment. He actually liked seeing his name at the top of the board. After all, it had been his dream when he started working for the company.

Somehow, Billy thought, *if I understand what the Barton's have been saying about thoughts being vibrations, it means I am attracting success to myself by the thoughts I think. If this is the case and my success isn't just happenchance, then I ought to be able to continually duplicate this performance just by controlling my thoughts.*

This idea excited Billy. He smiled to himself as he glanced back at the leader board. As he saw his name at the top again, he immediately felt a gush of pride and joy flow through him. He did love it at the top. What he wasn't sure of was the attention he would get from the others. He knew he would like having their respect, but he would rather not make it a big deal.

As Billy continued to look at the board, he remembered Yanis' words. "Billy, you recognize and act on your feelings. That is very special. It is the part of you that allows Kaula-O."

Yanis was right, he thought. *I know I love the feeling of being at the top. So I need to continue doing whatever is necessary to stay there.*

Billy finished at the office and left for the farm. He

had a boat to rebuild.

It was just before eight a.m. when Billy pulled up the driveway.

Goose got up and took a step forward to bark, but the bark never came. It was just Billy, so she lay back down.

Getting out of the car, he quickly made his way to the barn. Yanis was standing over the next piece of wood they needed to install.

"Good morning, Billy," the old man said. "I hope you slept well. How are Dana and the kids?"

"They are doing very well, thank you, Mr. Barton," Billy replied. "Dana and I talked for a long time last night. I tried to remember everything you and Mrs. Barton told me about Alexander's teachings. Dana was sure excited."

"Well, I have a special request," Yanis said. "Why don't you call me Yanis and Mrs. Barton, Izzy? We've heard about enough of this Mr. and Mrs. Barton stuff."

"Yes, Sir, Mr. Barton, err, Yanis," Billy replied.

"Thank you. Now, let's sit for a few moments before we start on the boat. There is a bit more to the story I would like to share with you before we get involved elsewhere."

Billy and Yanis stepped over to the familiar chairs sitting beside the wall. They sat and Yanis started the story, "It seems, Izzy, Alexander and I were still sitting on the porch after the storm. Alexander had just finished going through some more of his teachings when Izzy asked if I would like to take a bath.

"'Sure,' I told her. Not knowing what she had in mind. I guess I hadn't even thought of a bath since the storm started.

"She took my hand and we walked around to the back of the hut, and what I saw, well, I tell you Billy, if the view out the front of the hut was the most phenomenal view I had ever seen, then what I saw from the back of the hut was a close second.

"A small stream flowed down the mountain and tumbled down the face of a six-foot-high, ten-foot-wide rock ledge, creating a perfectly proportioned waterfall cascading into a small clear pool. The pool was about twenty feet in diameter. On the right edge of the pool, the water spilled over into a small stream and then continued down the mountain, eventually making its way into the lagoon below. On the opposite side of the pool, the jungle grew all the way down to the edge of the water. On the close side, however, it was level, grassy and green.

"'Here is our bathing area,' Izzy said. She smiled in my direction then turned her back to me and quickly slipped out of her clothes before stepping into the pool.

Not believing her lack of modesty, I quickly followed her lead.

"The cool water was fabulous. We playfully chased each other around the pool, swimming from one side to the other. You know, Billy, I think I was having more fun than I can ever remember having before. This beautiful young woman was quickly stealing my heart, and I knew it. After about an hour of playing, we were both water logged. Having brought towels from the hut, we quickly dried off. Wrapped in the towels, we laid in the warm sun at the water's edge.

"Izzy told me her family lived on the larger island to the north, Mountain Island. The island we were on was called Water Island. Alexander lived on this island alone. Izzy had just arrived at Water Island for her visit with her grandfather when I drifted onto the scene. She usually stayed with Alexander for a week each month. Izzy's grandfather and grandmother had lived on Water Island for many years when Izzy's mother was born. Alexander moved the three of them to Mountain Island so her mother could be raised with the other village people. Everyone in the village loved it when Alexander brought his family to live on Mountain Island. His presence made life easier for the village people who needed his assistance. Alexander was sought after for his wisdom and healing abilities. He was always happy to help.

"After Izzy's mother reached adulthood and married Izzy's father, Alexander took his wife back to Water Island. They both loved it and chose to live the rest of their lives there. Izzy's grandmother passed away six months before I broke my arm in the storm. It was apparent Alexander missed his wife very much.

"Izzy's grandmother was buried in the meadow next to the hut. Her grave was positioned so her spirit could look out across the ocean and see the beautiful view.

"Every time Izzy came for her visit, she questioned her grandfather about how he was feeling. Every month he would tell her the same thing. 'I'm doing very well, Izzy, thank you. Don't worry about me because when my time to pass arrives, you will know.' Izzy didn't understand how she would know, but she never pressed the subject.

"As the sun dropped below the horizon, we stood up from the grass where we lay drying. After dressing, Izzy took my hand and led me to the front porch. We found Alexander sitting in his chair watching the final moments of the sunset. From this vantage point, it was breathtaking. The sky seemed to reach out forever toward the west.

"Looking into the meadow, Izzy saw the fresh flowers Alexander put on her grandmother's grave. 'The flowers are beautiful, Grandfather,' she said, stepping up beside Alexander.

"'Yes they are,' he replied. 'You two look like you're having fun together,' his eyes gleaming in approval.

"'Yes, we have been having fun,' Izzy told him.

"'Tomorrow we should take that boat of yours and go fishing, Yanis,' Alexander suggested. 'That is, if you're not leaving tomorrow.' He glanced my way and offered a questioning look.

"It was at that point I realized leaving was the farthest thing from my mind. Why, I hadn't even thought of leaving.

"'Well, Sir,' I said, 'I would love to go fishing tomorrow if you don't mind me staying a bit longer.

"'Of course we don't,' Izzy jumped in with excitement. 'We would love you to stay as long as you want.'

"Alexander smiled at his granddaughter's eagerness to have me stay. I think it was obvious to him we were growing very close.

"The following day the weather was perfect. I felt

like I was in paradise. We had fruit for breakfast. Then Izzy and I went down the mountain to prepare the boat for our fishing trip. Alexander said he would be along shortly.

"It was midway through a rising tide, a perfect time to cross the shoal. This would give us six hours to fish and still have plenty of water on the outgoing tide when we returned. Alexander arrived as I finished getting the boat ready.

"He swam out to where we sat at anchor, holding a crocodile skin pack in one hand high above the water.

"'Where are the fishing rods?' I questioned.

"'I have what we need to catch the bigheaded fish,' he said.

"I assured him my boat was ready for the fishing adventure. But without fishing rods, I had my doubts.

"I released the sails and stepped forward on the deck to show Izzy how to hoist the anchor. In the cockpit, I pulled on the halyard and the mainsail rose up the mast.

"'We are free,' Izzy said as she lifted the chain rode and anchor up onto the deck.

"I pulled the tiller hard to starboard and the boat spun around. As she picked up speed, I watched over the side at the sandy bottom of the lagoon. The bottom gradually rose as we got closer to the shoal. A few moments later, we were across the sand bar.

"I looked at my watch. It was ten' o'clock. We sailed out and entered the Pacific Ocean. The waves were small. The wind was perfect, about fifteen knots. I turned south and sailed the boat parallel to the beach, just outside the line of small breakers. With the wind on her beam, we took off as if flying through the water.

"Alexander was standing in the cockpit with me. He had a look of pure joy in his eyes. He was at home on the ocean. My boat was very different compared to the small sailing catamarans the islanders used. But the principle was the same. You could tell Alexander absolutely loved where he was at that moment.

"He opened his crocodile pack and removed a large black spool of fishing line. He set it on the cockpit seat. Being intent on sailing the boat, I didn't see what he was doing until he was finished securing his lure to his line.

"'You have to be kidding,' I said, laughing at the old Kahuna's lure when he held it up for me to see. He had threaded his fishing line through a four-inch hollow reed about the size of a soda straw. Then he tied a treble fishing hook to the line and pulled the shank of the hook into the end of the reed. That was all there was to his fishing lure.

"'That will never work,' I said, continuing to laugh at his contraption.

"He smiled my direction and let the lure drop into the water beside the boat. As he fed the line out, he slowly jerked it back and forth in a quick motion. Finally, when the line was out as far as he wanted, he attached a large rubber band to the line and secured it to a stanchion on the boat.

"'Won't take long now,' he said, confidently looking in my direction.

"I just smiled and kept sailing the boat with a 'know it all' grin.

"Wham! The rubber band snapped tight and stretched

to almost breaking. I looked back toward the lure and there jumping high in the air was a beautiful greenish blue bull Dorado.

"'The bigheaded fish,' Alexander screamed. He grabbed the spool and released the rubber band from the line. He used his right arm as a shock absorber every time the fish took a jump. Cautiously he played with the fish, allowing it to jump high in the air and run back and forth across the water. As the big fish tired, he slowly wrapped the line around the spool and brought the Dorado to the boat. Reaching back into his pack, he took out a small knife. He reached over the side of the boat and cut the Dorado free.

"'That was fun, but the fish was too large,' he said. 'We have no way to keep such a large amount of meat fresh. I will catch a small one, one that will feed us for just a few days. That bigheaded fish was old and proud. He deserves to be free.

"I'm telling you, Billy, that was the largest bull Dorado I had ever seen. I bet it weighted seventy pounds. The old man pulled it in on a hand line like it was nothing.

"Alexander looked my way and quietly asked, 'Do you like my fancy fishing lure, now?' Now he was the one with the 'know it all' grin.

"I shook my head at his humor and admitted he had me that time.

"Alexander smiled back, prepared another reed lure and reset the fishing line. I, in turn, memorized exactly how he made it.

"It took all of about five minutes to catch a much

smaller Dorado. About fifteen pounds, I guess.

"'This one ought to last us a few days,' he said. 'It's time to go home.'

"We turned the boat around and headed toward shore. We were gone for less than an hour. The tide would be great with even more water over the shoal than when we left.

"'Yanis,' Izzy said on our way back into the lagoon. 'You never call your boat by name. You just refer to her as your boat. Why doesn't she have a name like most other boats?'

"'Well,' I told her. 'I've been calling her 'my boat' for so long, it's like it is her name.

"'I think we should name her something different,' she said. 'She deserves a pretty name.'

"'Oh, you think she deserves a pretty name, do you?' I questioned. I liked that Izzy was partial to my boat. I liked her interest in it. In fact, I liked everything I knew about Izzy. 'We'll talk about her name later,' I told her.

"We were in the cut and anchored by 11:30. Alexander cleaned and skinned the Dorado. The meat was wrapped in paper and he carried it back to the hut in his pack.

"Izzy and I stayed behind to clean and secure the boat. With the chores finished, I reached into a locker, retrieved a large hammock and carried it forward. I tied one end of the hammock chord to the headstay and wrapped the other end around the mast. I then stretched a canvas bimini above it for shade. I stepped up and sat in the hammock and laid back.

"'Come join me,' I suggested to Izzy.

"'Will it hold us both?' she asked.

"'Never fear,' I told her.

"She crawled into the hammock next to me. We both rolled over, looking into each other's eyes. She took my hand in hers.

"'I've been waiting a long time for someone like you,' she told me. 'My heart is singing.'

"'I know what you mean,' I responded. 'I feel the same way. I am falling in love with you.'

"'There is no more falling necessary for me,' she replied. 'I am there. I love you, Yanis Barton,' she simply said.

"I kissed Izzy for the first time that afternoon. It was the most beautiful thing I had ever done. There was truly no place I would rather have been than laying next to Izzy.

"We lay in that hammock all afternoon.

"Finally, Izzy suggested, 'If we hurry, we can make it to the pool before dark. A good fresh water swim will be so refreshing.'

"Remembering Izzy's way of swimming, the offer was too good to pass up. I quickly agreed.

"It was a great evening. I, Yanis Barton, was in love.

"The next two days were perfect. Izzy and I grew closer and closer. One afternoon as we were lying by the pool, I asked her if any of the village women ever left Mountain Island to marry.

"'Yes,' she replied. 'Sometimes they do. Sometimes they fall in love with men from other islands.'

"'Do you ever think that would be something you

might do?' I asked her, holding my fingers crossed.

"'Do you mean leave the island with you, Yanis?' she probed, looking straight into my eyes.

"I looked back into those big beautiful brown eyes. 'Yes, Izzy, that's exactly what I mean. Will you marry me and go back to the United States as my wife?'

"'Yanis, I have tried to slow my emotions, to take my time. But that has not happened. I think I might have known the first day I saw you that this was going to happen. But I didn't know it would happen so quickly. I have only known you for a week, but it seems like we have been together for so much longer. Yes, Yanis, I will marry you. I would love to be your wife.' Then, she added with deep sincerity, 'I can't just leave my grandfather. Not yet.'

"'That is good enough for me,' I told her. 'As long as I'm with you I can be anywhere we need to be.'

"I leaned down and tenderly kissed my future wife's lips. I was so in love, Billy. I thought my chest would explode with emotion.

"We couldn't wait to tell Grandfather. We walked around to the front of the hut and found him kneeling in front of the fire pit. He had just finished grilling the last of the Dorado. Boy did it smell good. I was hungry.

"'Grandfather,' Izzy said as we approached him hand in hand, both smiling. 'We have something to tell you.'

"'You are coming to tell me that you are getting married, and you want me to bless your union,' Alexander said without looking up.

"'You knew?' Izzy said.

"'How could one not know?" Alexander questioned, taking his eyes off the fish and smiling at his granddaughter.

"'It is true. Yanis has asked me to marry him,' Izzy replied.

"'And you said?' her grandfather asked, leaning in Izzy's direction.

"'I said yes, of course. I love him so much."

"'And does Yanis love you the same?' he asked, looking my direction.

"'I love your granddaughter, Alexander. I will love her and protect her forever. May I marry Izzy?' I asked.

"'You have made me the happiest grandfather in the world. Your marriage has been blessed for a very long time. Yanis, I thank you for coming for my granddaughter. You have answered my dream. I am proud for both of you. This has been my wish for a very long time and the timing could not be more perfect.'

"Alexander took Izzy's hand and suggested we step near where her grandmother was buried. He felt this was a happy day that should be shared with her.

"'About a year ago, your grandmother and I stood on the porch. We looked out across the large expanse of ocean. She said, 'It will be a wonderful day when the man Izzy loves comes to get her. Someone who can take her places she has never been. The world and our islands are changing. It is my dream for Izzy. She would do well out there,' she said, pointing out to sea.

"'Your grandmother and I felt very much the same

way. We both wanted you to have this opportunity. The seed of the dream we shared on that day was backed with such joy. And now that dream has come to fruition. Your grandmother would be pleased.'

"The three of us stood there for a moment and embraced each other. Alexander was a happy man."

At this point in the story, Yanis was still seated in the barn. He stopped speaking and stood to stretch.

"Billy," he said. "Alexander taught Izzy and me many things about the old-world teachings. But the primary thing I want you to understand is this: once you realize that your thoughts create, then learn to direct that creation by thinking thoughts that bring forth the results you want. This process allows you to be the director of your life. Just imagine what wonderful results you can achieve directing the circumstances of your life by controlling your thoughts. Your life will become whatever you choose to make it. And, my young friend, it doesn't take that long to accomplish. Major changes can occur very quickly."

"Really?" Billy questioned.

"Yes, really. Just remember the steps we spoke of yesterday. Clearly imagine your dream while backing it with positive emotions. Then have faith and believe in the process by staying focused on the intention through positive action. A good way to do this is by visualizing your dream daily as already accomplished and acting positively toward that outcome. This will fuel the dream with emotions and feelings of successful accomplishment. But only do this for a few moments each day. Billy, it's hard to keep your mind from wandering, especially at first. As soon as you have felt the emotional charge of success and gratitude, move your mind to something else. Don't give it time to wander into thoughts of doubt or disbelief. And the third and final step is, you must accept the fulfillment of the dream into your life. This is often the hardest step of the three and may require repetitive imagining over and over before acceptance can occur. Be tenacious and don't give up. Because, in this repetition, Alexander taught, limiting beliefs would dissolve and acceptance could occur.

"In my life I have seen this process work over and over again. It is something I have learned I can count on. The more you experience success with the process the more you will expect it, then the more expectant you are the quicker you receive."

Billy looked at Yanis as though he understood and the old man continued. "Alexander taught that the imagining process could benefit from a visual aid. Instead of just imagining his dream or desire, he often painted a simple picture of what he wanted. Even though to you and me his painting may have no resemblance to our interpretation of what he desired, that didn't matter. He knew each and every mark or stroke he made. Each had a meaning of its own. The paintings would all include a stickman with a ring in his left ear. That was Alexander's representation of himself. He always wore a silver hoop in his left ear, like a pirate.

"Billy, come with me for a moment. I want to show you something," Yanis said, leading Billy to a small storage room in the back of the barn. He walked over to an old chest and pulled out a weathered backpack made of crocodile skin.

Billy assumed it was Alexander's old backpack. He looked at Yanis for confirmation.

"All these years it's been stored here," Yanis said. "Alexander gave it to Izzy before he passed. Let me see if what I'm looking for is still inside." Yanis opened the pack and removed two small paintings. In one picture, a stick man with long gray hair and a silver ring in his left ear stood on the porch of a small hut. He appeared to be looking down the side of a mountain at the ocean. Far out to sea was the white triangular sail of a sailboat.

"This was Alexander's image of his desire for someone to come for his granddaughter," Yanis explained. "He drew the painting shortly after his wife passed."

"What about the other painting?" Billy asked.

Yanis held up the other painting. It showed the familiar stickman with the ring in his ear standing on the beach. There was a small sailboat floating just inside the lagoon. Standing in knee-deep water was a stickman with short blonde hair and a stick woman with long black hair, shaking hands. Billy looked at it for a moment.

"Was this supposed to be you and Izzy when you met?" he asked.

"That is what Alexander said," Yanis confirmed. "He showed us these paintings the day we told him of our desire to get married. He felt they were instrumental in manifesting his desire of Izzy finding a man that would take her from the South Pacific. Looking at them helped him feel the emotional charge of joy and gratitude of successfully achieving his dream. As I've said before, these are two of the most powerful emotions one can feel.

"I have learned the importance of using pictures or photos of my desires. The visual stimulus crystallizes the desire in my mind. I have also seen the power in writing down my desires in a planner. By writing down my desires, I can be very clear and precise as to what my dreams are. Both of these actions have a tremendous effect toward achieving what it is I want from life.

"Billy, Alexander taught that imagining a dream or goal in your mind is all that is really necessary. But to see a clear and precise picture of it offers added stimulation, especially if the picture is from your point of view. In the fulfillment of your dreams, you find joy and contentment. As this takes place, your expectancy grows into acceptance and the process is complete. Your dream is fulfilled." Yanis hesitated for a moment. "Billy, do you have a planner?"

"Yes, Sir," Billy answered. "I have a simple one the company gave me when I started."

"Do you use it?" the old man asked.

"Well, I guess I don't use it very often," Billy returned. "I don't have many appointments. My schedule is not very busy."

"There is magic in using a planner. I would suggest you start using yours. Would you mind if I took a quick look at your planner?" Yanis asked him. "I don't want to be snoopy, but I want to show you how to use it."

"Not at all," Billy told him. "It's in the car. I'll get it."

Returning to the barn, Billy handed his planner to Yanis.

"I don't intend to stick my nose into your business. But, can I ask you something?" Yanis questioned.

"Certainly," Billy said.

"What would be your greatest desire right now?" Yanis asked.

Billy had to think only briefly before stating, "My overall dream is to have a very successful, happy life here in Colorado with my family. But my immediate desire is to bring my family home."

"I figured you would say that," Yanis confirmed. "And I have heard you say that you and Dana have attached a monetary amount that you both feel is necessary before the dream can be fulfilled."

"Yes, Sir," Billy said. "The income is absolutely essential."

"Okay," Yanis agreed. "I understand your situation and the importance the money plays. So with this attachment to your dream, let's concentrate on its accomplishment for the moment, okay? I will show you a few simple steps that greatly enhanced my career when I was in my early production years, just the same as you are now. When Izzy and I returned to the states from Water Island, my first job was in sales. I learned very quickly to use a planner similar to this one, except I added another single page to it.

"I took a piece of typing paper and taped a series of pictures on the upper half of the paper. Each picture was an image of a particular goal I had, whether it was a new car, a certain sales level I wanted to achieve, or whatever; that is, if I could find a picture that represented my goal. It was a long time ago when I first started applying Alexander's techniques. A camera and film was pretty rare. Most of the time, my desires were things you might find in a Sears and Roebuck catalog. I could cut out a new dress for Izzy or a new suit for myself and tape them on the paper. Now it seems everyone has a camera, making this process much easier.

"But, in a situation like yours, if your goal is the return of your family, I suggest you get a picture of the four of you together and tape it in the upper left hand corner of your piece of paper. Under the picture, write a powerful statement that will positively charge the dream or the goal. In this example, I would write something like, 'Living with my wife and children fills my life with joy and happiness.' It's important to word the phrases properly. Alexander taught it was best to write them as thought they were already accomplished.

"Now let's address the savings goal you feel you need for their return. Take a copy of your current bank statement. Reduce it down to fit on the middle upper section of the paper. Whiteout the number that has dwindled to nothing and fill in the goal number you desire. Then under that picture write your powerful statement proving your expectancy.

"You can put as many pictures or visual aids on the goal paper as you choose. I would fill the upper three quarters of the paper with your goals. Then, down along the bottom of the page, draw four squares. The first square can be your weekly production goal and the number that corresponds to that goal. The second can be your monthly production goal with its corresponding number. Let's say the third is your annual production goal and its corresponding number. The fourth box I call the Magic Moment Goal and I will explain it in a moment.

"After you get your goals written down, place the paper inside your planner on the present day. Each day after reading and imagining your goals as if they have already been achieved, move the paper forward to the following day. Now, Billy, every day refer to your planner," Yanis stated, emphasizing 'every day.' "Focus on each goal as you look at the picture and the statement. Feel the emotional charge of success and joyful appreciation of each goal as though already accomplished. Then move the paper to the next day. Keep these weekly, monthly and annual goals high enough to offer challenge, but not so high you consciously discount them as impossible to reach, and thus give up. Set your goals at least equal to, if not just a bit greater than, your best prior achievement.

"The fourth box, your Magic Moment Goal, is different. Here, literally reach for the stars. Put a figure in this box that is two, three even four times the number in your annual goal square. Because Billy, it doesn't matter whether you make this goal or not. That takes all the pressure off. Your annual goal will be enough to provide for your family. The Magic Moment Goal should just be icing on the cake. Tear off the box with the Magic Moment Goal and put it in your wallet. Every time you get into your wallet glance at the paper. Billy, I can tell you this: the word *magic* in the Magic Moment Goal is real. It won't take very long for you to realize the Magic Moment Goal is just as real as the first three production goals. Since it's stashed away in your wallet, you tend to forget about it. When you least expect it, it is accomplished.

"When your goals start to come forth, take notice and begin to witness truly phenomenal events. The events will give you unparalleled emotional joy. As the emotions of joy and appreciation arise, the more success you will attract to appreciate. The vibrations of these positive feelings continue to attract extraordinary things into your life. That's why I called them the Magic Moment Goals. They are life changers.

"Here is an important thing to remember. As you direct your life by controlling your thoughts, you need to stay attentive by intentionally directing your thoughts down a positive path. The most powerful vibration comes when you completely expect the manifestation of your dreams. This becomes natural through your experience of success. You will begin to watch large dreams unfold within a short period of time. Basically, when you no longer have to try to think power thoughts, but instead they come naturally, the effectiveness of the thoughts will become even more evident.

"Tonight when you get home, write down your goals. Since you said earlier that you had only ninety days to reach your important monetary goal, let's just work on projecting your goals out for ninety days. Take your pictures, your bank statement or whatever visual aid you want to use and tape them on the upper part of the paper. Now, write down your weekly, monthly, annual and Magic Moment Goal. Then, tear off the corner box with the Magic Moment Goal from the paper and put it inside your wallet. Every time you open your wallet and see the number in the box, take a moment to smile, feeling the joy of this goal being accomplished. Then, close the wallet and forget it. We'll talk about that number in ninety days. Okay, are you willing to try this?"

"I sure am," Billy stated without any hesitancy.

Yanis added. "Just remember, what you desire backed with positive emotion and fully expected by you is brought forth into reality. It is the process, Alexander taught. There is no chance and there is no luck involved. The sizes of the goals or dreams you achieve are only dependent upon the size of your belief that they can come true. But remember, Billy. It's what you believe on the inside that counts, what your Unihipilili or your lower self believes. Alexander taught one of the ways your lower self learns is through repetition of exposure whether real or imagined. So if you continue to present it with imagined situations as though already accomplished, backed with emotion, it's limiting beliefs will change. If you look at your goals every day and stay focused on your intention for complete success through positive thought and action, the acceptance of their completion will come naturally. Situations around you will begin to change in ways necessary to allow the fulfillment of these goals. Have fun with this, Billy. Life is about joy. That knowledge alone will take you a long way. We will talk further about this tomorrow, if you can return."

Yanis looked at his watch. They had been talking all morning. "It's almost noon. So, you know who will be coming through that door in just a few moments?"

"Yes I do, and we haven't done a thing on the boat today," Billy commented.

"Billy," Yanis stated firmly, "what we've been talking about could possibly be the most beneficial information you will ever be presented with. That boat can wait another day."

Sure enough, Izzy came walking through the door.

"Lunch is served," she said, setting the tray of food on the table. "Should I ask what you boys have been talking about?"

"I was telling Billy about the personal planner you and I used for so many years. He's going to give it a try," Yanis replied.

"I suppose you had him include the Magic Moment Goal," she said.

"Yes, I sure did."

"Then I only hope he's ready for you know what, the 'Prosperity Train.'"

They all got a laugh out of her comment. Billy finished lunch in silence, trying to remember every detail of what Yanis had told him. Promising to return the next day, he drove straight home.

Billy took a blank sheet of paper out of his briefcase and started drawing his squares along the bottom. He tallied his goals for each and wrote them in the boxes. As he wrote the numbers, he tried to imagine joyfully how he would feel when each goal was accomplished. When he got to the Magic Moment goal, he hesitated. He remembered Yanis saying to "dream big." *Now is no time to be logical,* Billy thought. He wrote a number down that truly seemed to be reaching for the stars. Tearing off the box, he put it inside his wallet. He smiled at himself when he remembered Yanis explain just how real this goal was because *fulfilling this goal would really take some Magic.*

Next, he took a picture of his family and taped it on the top of the paper. Then he did the bank statement just as Yanis suggested. He later took a picture of the sales board with his name in the top position. Billy made small visual aids for each goal he desired and taped them on the paper. Now he wrote power statements under each one. As he wrote each statement, he felt excited. He could immediately feel a charge of expectancy. Then he folded the paper and put it in the planner for the next day.

He quickly called Dana and shared the day's events. Then Billy prepared for his evening appointments.

Arriving at his first appointment early, he sat outside in his car thinking about the two sales presentations he made the night before last when both were successful. He held that image clearly in his mind and then tried to feel the emotional high his success created.

Could it really be this easy? Billy thought. *He remembered Yanis saying it's what you believe on the inside that counts. Repitition is the key. Yanis said to think happy thoughts when you imagine your dreams.* So, Billy determined, tonight would be the same as the night before. He closed his eyes and thought about his family. His children always made him smile. He loved them so much. They always gave him a happy heart. Then, with this joyful emotion running through his mind, Billy focused on his appointments being successful. He tried to clearly see and feel the joy of a win-win experience for both him and his customers.

Later that night, Billy went home smiling. He was a successful salesperson and proud of it. The two new sales orders in his briefcase were still more proof that Billy was on his way.

7

THE GARDEN

The seeds of dreams can prosper when
Provided love and care,
With joyful feelings you can send
The thoughts you want to share.

The following morning, Billy opened his planner while he ate breakfast. He looked at his goal sheet. Starting in the upper left hand corner, he looked at his visual aid and read the power statement below it while feeling the joy of achieving the goal. He then felt appreciation for the dream as if it had been accomplished.

When he got to the bottom of the page and read through his weekly, monthly and ninety-day goals, he smiled to himself. *My how life has changed this week*, he thought. *Just Sunday Dana and I had figured I needed to make seventy sales in ninety days to achieve the monetary goals we agreed upon for her and the children to return to Colorado. But now that I have already made nineteen sales this week and I assume I will make two more this evening and two again tomorrow totaling twenty-three for the week, I wrote twenty-five as my weekly goal. That made one hundred for my monthly goal and three hundred for the ninety-day goal. That was a far cry from the seventy I originally needed.*

Then Billy laughed out loud when he remembered what he wrote for his Magic Moment Goal and slipped into his wallet the night before. In his mind he took the fifteen he sold to the Bartons and multiplied it times five days a week, four weeks a month, times three months and came up with the number nine hundred. Billy got so excited thinking about this number that he stood up from the kitchen table and started dancing around the room singing, "nine hundred, nine hundred, nine hundred."

I just figure if I'm going to dream I might as well dream first class; no need to dream economy, Billy thought before sitting back down to finish his bowl of cereal.

Billy slipped his goal sheet to the next day, remembering Yanis' instructions of not dwelling on the dreams for very long to avoid letting doubt creep into his thoughts.

As Billy arrived at the office to turn in his prior evening's sales agreements, he saw his manager sitting behind his desk talking with another man. Billy quickly moved on to the large central office where the phones were located. Just as he began to sit down, he heard his manager call his name.

"Billy, Billy McCoy, could you please come into my office, I would like you to meet someone," his manager said, sticking his head out his office door.

"Sure," Billy replied, not knowing what this could be about. He quickly walked into the manager's private office.

"Billy, I would like to introduce Les Harvey. Les is the regional manager in charge of sales. He works in the main office in Denver. That order you turned in yesterday caught his eye. He came down here to congratulate you personally on your sales performance. As you know, the salespeople employed here, as well as statewide, seem to average around six to eight sales agreements per week. Sometimes someone will get real lucky and reach ten. But that is very seldom. In fact, Billy, the most any salesperson has ever turned in for a week of production, companywide, is eighteen. Since you turned in seventeen sales agreements within the first few days of the week, Les wanted to see if he could urge you on a bit. He wants you to try and break our weekly record."

Billy stepped over and shook Mr. Harvey's hand. "It's a pleasure to meet you, Sir," he said.

"Billy, believe me the pleasure is all mine," Mr. Harvey returned. "We were just talking about how great it would be if the longstanding sales record was broken. Actually, I looked it up in the company records and found it has been in place for fifteen years. That is what stimulated me to come down and personally encourage you to break it. Just two more sales Billy and a new record will be in place. To entice you further, this morning I called the company's board of directors and suggested to them that anytime someone surpasses a company record, even by one sale, they would qualify for a bonus of one thousand dollars. The board agreed completely and approved the idea. I thought I would personally come down and offer you this challenge. What do you think, Billy?"

Billy didn't really know what to think. He hadn't seen more than twenty-four sales by one sales person on the board in any given month. So, looking at his achievement from that perspective, eighteen in one week was quite a feat. Billy felt that gush of pride surface again, but his humble nature came through.

"Mr. Harvey," Billy replied, "I think you can be certain that old record will fall." Billy cleared his throat and continued. "I had two more appointments last evening. They were both successful. I came into the office this morning to turn in two more sales." Billy, now realizing he was still carrying his briefcase, reached in and produced the two sales agreements, handing them to Mr. Harvey.

"Somehow, I feel like I just got set up. That was just too easy," Mr. Harvey said, smiling at Billy in jest. "Not really, son. Seriously, you should be very proud of yourself. Just how high do you think you will take your sales production this month?"

Before Billy could answer, Mr. Harvey spoke up again. "It doesn't really matter, Billy. Even if you sell no more over the next three weeks, it is still a very successful month for you. I intend to come down next week and personally present you with a bonus check at your weekly sales meeting. Would that be alright with you?" Mr. Harvey directed the question toward Billy's manager for confirmation.

"That would be wonderful," the manager said. "Billy, my boy, you are on your way to a fine career. I'm proud to have you working with us."

Mr. Harvey agreed.

Billy was feeling overwhelmed and was becoming a bit anxious with all the attention. He realized there would be even more attention next week at the sales meeting. He quickly thanked the two managers and quietly left the office. The thousand dollars was a real bonus. Billy knew he and Dana could sure use it. *Maybe he could handle a thousand dollars worth of attention*, he acknowledged to himself.

While driving home, something occurred to Billy. Yanis suggested Billy set his goals at least equal to if not greater than his very best prior achievement. To Billy, that meant having to achieve one hundred sales every month.

How could I ever hit that number every month? he thought. *It's just too high. I'll have to discuss it with Yanis. Surely, there needs to be some tolerance or adjustment.*

At home, Billy made his referral calls from the night before. Contacting referrals was one of the more rewarding things this job offered. Billy found that when his new customers were excited and happy with their purchase, the referrals they shared with him were the same. The friends of his customers often had similar attitudes and thus were happy and easy to work with. After he set two appointments for that evening, it was time he left for the farm. It was already ten o'clock. Yanis would need some help.

That morning after his coffee, instead of going straight to the barn, Yanis decided to help Izzy in her garden. She was happy for his offer. There were beans and squash and various other things needing to be picked. After a couple of hours, when they each had a full sack of vegetables, they sat down on the shady side of a tall row of sweet corn growing on the edge of the garden.

"Life can't get much better than this, can it?" Izzy suggested. "Look at all this beautiful food we grow ourselves. Aren't you proud of our productive farm that feeds so many families?"

"It's a good life we have created," Yanis agreed. "We have been most fortunate. By the way, did you send down the request for the complete purchase of the employee gifts? I want to make sure we get it approved at the next board meeting."

"Yes, I logged it onto their agenda," Izzy replied. "But that won't be until next month."

"Yes, I know," Yanis responded.

About that time Goose, who was laying in the shade of the corn beside them, sounded off her one-bark alarm.

"That must be Billy," Yanis said as he stood to walk around the barn toward the house. You sit tight. I'll bring him back here. He can help us carry the full sacks of vegetables to the front porch. It'll give you a chance to show off this wonderful garden of yours."

"I'll be right here," she said, keeping her seat in the shade.

Yanis walked around the side of the barn. Billy was just getting out of his car.

"Hey, Billy. Come around here for a moment. I need your help."

Billy followed the old man back to the garden.

"Hello, Billy," Izzy waved at him. "Here I am, sitting down on the job."

"By the size of those sacks, I'd say you already finished your job," Billy returned. "What a marvelous garden; I didn't know this was back here."

"Every year we grow a big garden. I wish I could take credit for it all myself, but I can't. Several of the employees do most of the hard work."

"How do you ever eat all the food that comes out of a garden this size?" Billy asked.

"Oh my, we couldn't eat all this," Izzy swept her hand across the expanse of her garden. "Actually, we give most of the food away. There are plenty of takers for fresh produce. The homeless shelters in town are the recipients of most of it."

Billy just smiled. Why was he not surprised? These were the most caring people he had ever met.

"Come here, Billy," Izzy requested. "Let me give you a close-up tour of my wonderful garden." Izzy took Billy's hand. She led him to the far end of the garden, stopping ever so often to point out a particularly special something or other. Yanis sat back down in the shade and waited with Goose.

After a few moments, the two made their way back to Yanis and they both sat down in the shade.

"Are we going to remove the first piece of wood from the rail and glue it back in place today?" Billy asked.

"I think that is the next step," Yanis replied. "It shouldn't take us very long since the holes are all pre-drilled."

"Could I ask you a question before we get started?" Billy asked. "I've been a bit confused this morning about the way you suggested I set my goal figures."

"Certainly," Yanis returned. "Ask away, Billy."

"Well, yesterday you said to determine the number I enter into each box, I should pick a number at least equal to or greater than the highest level of prior achievement for that box."

"Yes, I did say that," Yanis agreed.

"Well," Billy said. "Yesterday, I drove home and drew my boxes and filled them all with numbers based on my family's income needs. Then, for the Magic Moment Goal I really zoomed out there. I put in a huge number. I even smiled at myself realizing just how much of your magic it would take to fulfill. But this morning as I was driving, I mentally calculated what would happen if my production level continued. So far, I have your fifteen and four more individual sales. That is in less than a week, which incidentally qualified me for a great bonus I should thank you folks for. I broke a fifteen-year sales record for the company. So what that means, if I am successful tonight on my two appointments and continue that same success pattern for the balance of the month, my total monthly production should be around a hundred. That number is almost four times the highest amount ever produced in one month by a salesperson in our company."

Yanis sat there intently listening to Billy.

Billy waited for his reply. No reply came. Izzy didn't even say a word.

After what seemed an eternity, but in fact was only a few seconds, Billy spoke again. "Don't you see what I am talking about?" he said, shaking his head with concern.

"Well, Billy, I do agree the numbers appear correct," Yanis agreed. "But I don't understand where the problem is. I thought you wanted to make a lot of sales?"

"I do," replied Billy. "But one hundred in one month. No one has ever done that before."

"Oh, I see what you are saying," Yanis returned with a smile. "You feel the number one hundred is too large to accomplish in a month. Billy, think about this. A few days ago, I bet nineteen in a week was a number that to you appeared too large to accomplish," the old man hesitated briefly, then continued. "But it wasn't, was it?"

Billy shook his head. He saw the old man's point, but before he could respond, Yanis continued. "There are two points we discussed prior that apply here. The first is this: you will only receive in life what you expect to receive. If one hundred is a number you wish to focus on, see it clearly in your mind. Then, even if only for the briefest moment, charge it with the emotion of absolute success. Feel the joy of that success and the thrill of its accomplishment. Now, move your thinking away. Put your mind on something else. Do not allow logic to step in and begin to sell you into thinking one hundred is too large a number. Direct your thinking and you direct your life. Now, the second point we spoke of is this: often the imagination part of your dream is the simplest and the harder part is found in the expectancy and the acceptance of your dream into reality."

Billy nodded affirmatively. "I remember you saying that yesterday," he said.

"Most people live their lives like this," Yanis continued, "they have a dream and feel the excitement of its accomplishment, or in other words, they plant the seeds. But, then they dwell on the dream too long and allow the negative thoughts to surface. They logically prove to themselves that the dream is impossible. The seeds they just planted now begin to wither away. What they discover is that in their case their logic was correct. So their feelings of defeat are allowed to prosper as their dominate feeling and create their reality."

"When you have seen this process work over and again," Izzy said, addressing Billy, "your expectancy becomes automatic. It is very easy to believe and therefore accept your dream into reality once you have seen this method work. When you are new to these teachings, it takes some effort to have faith of expectancy. Let me give you an example."

Izzy motioned toward the tall row of corn next to them.

"Last spring we decided we wanted fresh corn to eat this fall. Understanding the cycle of growth, we planted seeds of corn in our garden. Now we needed to nourish the seeds and protect them. We gave them water and not too much sunlight. We kept the insects out of the field and we kept the weeds away from the stalks. If you were a young child and didn't know or understand the process of growing a plant how would you ever believe that a seed would grow forth into a tall stalk of corn?"

"Well, you would have to take someone's word for it, I guess," Billy answered.

"That is right," Izzy continued. "Really, the only way to gain faith in the process is to have faith in the one who tells it to you, or have the experience of seeing the growth for yourself, with your own eyes."

Billy nodded. "Yes, I see that."

"Okay, back to our seeds," Izzy spoke with a bit of excitement. "Within about a week we see small sprouts appear. What do you think the small child is thinking?"

"Well, I would think the child is beginning to believe in the possibility of the plants' growth," Billy replied, "because the child sees the small plants sprouting."

"Exactly," Izzy exclaimed. "Have you ever seen the reaction of a child the first time they see their seeds sprout? It's pure joy. And every day, as the plants grow taller and taller, it reinforces expectancy in the child's mind. It's the same as when you notice the small changes in your life that take place that opens the pathway to your dream fulfillment.

"Now, this is an important point, as the child's expectancy reaches its greatest level of faith in the growth process, complete belief occurs and the child accepts the dream into reality. They pick an ear of corn. So you see, Billy, the number 'one hundred' is like an ear of corn. It challenges your level of knowing. But just for the moment. Just the way planting a seed will challenge a child's belief that it can possibly become an ear of corn. The child will learn and gain confidence in the possibility as they see the plant grow larger and larger.

"You will gain confidence in the possibility of achieving your goal of one hundred sales as you recognize the smaller achievements that begin to happen from your goal sheet. As you see the goals become reality, Billy, it is very important that you acknowledge them and take notice. Be very appreciative. As you do, you will begin to expect the accomplishment of all your dreams and in turn become the director of your life. Your life is no longer being created through misdirection, confusion and happenchance."

Izzy smiled as she finished. "You are a good student, Billy. You ask all the right questions and listen very well."

Hearing Izzy's analogy of the cornstalk seemed to make it much easier for Billy to understand the process. He could definitely see how feelings of expectancy are not automatic, until a person has the benefit of a personal experience. He could also see the importance of recognizing even the smallest change in his life situation. Small steps form the pathway to the achievement of larger goals. Another big thing Billy noticed was that his thoughts never drifted toward financial failure anymore. His focus was on production numbers. Fear of insufficient income wasn't present the way it used to be.

Billy could also see a huge difference in his demeanor when he entered the office. He was no longer on the bottom of the sales board. Even if it was his first time to reach the top position on the board, it still gave him a feeling of being very successful. Billy, along with his manager, realized that the continued success he was having each evening was even more proof he was on his way.

"The sun is getting higher in the sky. Our shade is disappearing," Yanis said. "I think it's time we make like horses and head for the barn."

Billy picked up both sacks of vegetables and carried them to the front porch. Then he met Yanis in the barn for their boat chores.

That day's chore was simple. They merely undid what they had already done. They added sealant and glue and reinstalled the wood, permanently securing the first piece of caprail in place. The process only took an hour.

Just as they were finishing, Izzy showed up with lunch. It was quarter to twelve.

"Right on cue," Yanis winked toward Billy. "You'd think she was watching us or something. She always shows up just at the right time."

"I'm sure glad she does," Billy confessed, taking his chair in preparation.

"I've got time to help you put another piece of wood on the rail," he said. "That is, if you're up for it.

"Why don't we," Yanis agreed. "Then tomorrow we can do the same thing to the third piece and we'll be one day away from finishing the caprail on this side." All three realized they now took it for granted that Billy would return the next day. It made the old couple very happy and Billy loved it, too. He really did feel at home with them.

The next piece of wood took two full hours to install because they had to fit the two pieces together with a scarf joint then slightly bend it into place as they drilled the holes and inserted the bolts. Once it was in place, they stood back and admired their work. Again, it looked like it belonged on the boat.

It was well after two p.m. when they finished. Yanis was ready for his nap and Billy needed to be getting back to town to prepare for his evening appointments.

"One more thing," Yanis suggested before Billy left for his car. "You may tend to dwell on the thought that one hundred sales mean you need more than perfect success every night. If you get caught up in that feeling, move your mind off the thought. Break your goal down into smaller, simpler challenges. If all that is required is for you to have five successful appointments per day, then maybe you can figure out a way to make presentations to multiple couples at once. Or, better yet, why not make the presentation to a large group. It seems to me that for the same effort you might double or even triple your production. Just think what would happen if you met with several couples at the same time. Billy, sometimes establishing higher goals has its own magic. It often stimulates your creativity in new directions, new possibilities for success. I'll see you tomorrow."

Billy left for home thinking the entire time he drove about an appointment with five couples at once. How could he do that? The more he thought about it the more it appeared it might not be all that difficult. He loved talking on the phone with his referrals. They always seemed receptive to him. Why couldn't he simply ask each of the five couples if they could meet somewhere in common to listen to his presentation? *If I have presentations three times a week at specific times it would allow the couples optional times and days that may not conflict with their schedules*, he thought. But Billy knew that evenings were family times. Appointments at their homes allowed them to care for their families during the presentation. That is what made evening appointments so easy. *But, what about offering a free catered lunch?* he thought.

The more Billy thought about the idea, the more he liked it. *Some restaurants have private sections offered at no charge, and the restaurant could provide the food.* Billy was excited about his new idea. He started checking for the best restaurant options as soon as he got to the office.

He found that most restaurants offered private areas; however, to get a private area during peak hours they required at least ten couples before the restaurant would be willing to close down a section.

This presents another problem, Billy thought. He didn't have ten referrals. He only had four left from his previous customers. *However, after this evening's success, maybe I could get a few more. Funny choice of words,* he thought, *'after this evening's success.'* The thought had no hint of failure. Billy realized it came forth automatically. It had no trace of doubt.

If necessary, Billy might call his prior customers back, explain what he wanted to do and ask each if they would like to attend a free luncheon and bring a friend. *That was the answer,* Billy thought. *That was the new plan.* He would start the calls tomorrow after that evening's appointments.

8

TENDING THE GARDEN

So, see your dreams precise and clear
Give power with your thought,
Through faith believe your dream is here
Accept that which you sought.

It was Saturday, ending the first full week since Dana and the kids had gone back to her parents. The early morning rays of light filtered through the blinds in Billy's room. He lay in bed thinking about how much his life had changed in such a short time.

After just a week of production, he was a third of the way to the goal he and Dana set to be reached in three months. Putting the financial success aside, Billy felt there was another primary thing that had changed. He recognized smaller events happening around him. Events he could readily name, like his manager sharing the important leads a week ago. What an opportunity that was. Not to mention Les Harvey and the bonus check. Don't forget his friend who happened to have a place for him to live, as well as store his family's belongings. It all seemed to be working in his favor.

Almost like it was preplanned, he thought, smiling to himself at his choice of words. *This does feel great. I am happy and very grateful.*

Billy decided to go into the office long enough to turn in last evening's sales agreements. The office was open until noon on Saturday. Looking at his watch, he realized it was already 7:30. By the time he finished at the office and made it to the farm, it would be almost nine. Yanis would be ready to install the final piece of wood on the first side of the boat. With no appointments for the day, Billy was free to do as he pleased.

When Billy reached the office, he quickly gave the secretary the paperwork from the previous evening. Then he stepped into the large central office to get more blank forms.

When he entered the room, he noticed two salespeople standing beside the file cabinet where the forms were kept.

"Hi, Billy," one of them said as he approached. "Quite a stroke of good luck you had this week."

"Yes, I have been fortunate," Billy agreed.

"Being only a week into this month," the second salesperson said, "how many more sales are you trying for?"

Feeling the salespeople were genuinely interested in Billy's efforts, he answered, "I would like to get a clean one hundred."

"I think you're dreaming about that one," the first salesperson said with a snicker. "Your luck can't run that long. The only way to do that is to pick up another huge sale like the one you got this week. And those are once in a lifetime."

"I wouldn't expect that to happen again," the second confirmed. "If everything worked out perfectly, you might hit fifty." The two salespeople walked away, leaving Billy feeling let down and unsupported.

Billy knew why they thought one hundred sales seemed impossible; just yesterday, he had a bucket full of doubt himself. Billy realized his perspective had changed since Yanis' suggestion of the multiple couples at each presentation. His focus was no longer on the large number of one hundred, but instead on the smaller number of prospective customers attending his luncheon appointments.

It was time to go to the farm. He'd had enough of the office.

Yanis was already in the barn when Billy arrived. "Sorry I'm late," he said. "Had to stop by the office and turn in a couple agreements."

"That's getting to be a habit, isn't it?" Yanis asked cheerfully.

"Yes, and a good habit it is," Billy confirmed with a smile. "I was lying in bed this morning thinking of all the small things that have changed in my life this past week. It seems everything is working in my favor. I feel like I want to tell someone how much I appreciate all this good fortune, but don't know who to tell."

"Just feel it, Billy," Yanis said. "Just feel it and it will get to the right place. As a matter of fact, it already is."

"I know," Billy replied. "Here comes the 'Prosperity Train.'"

Yanis laughed. "You're learning. Let's get this third piece of wood in place, what do you think?"

The third piece of wood took a little less time to install because the hull was straight at the stern of the boat and the wood didn't need to be bent. They drilled the holes and then immediately removed the wood and reinstalled it with sealant and glue. Securing the bolts below deck completed this side of the boat.

"Yanis," Billy said, "this morning when I went into the office I ran into two salespeople and we had a short conversation. They asked how many total sales I intended to produce this month. I thought they were genuinely interested so I told them my goal was one hundred. Well, they were anything but supportive. Basically, they said it was impossible. They felt maybe fifty could be achieved, but never one hundred. At first, I was shocked at their response. But then I remembered how I initially felt. So I completely understand their feelings. But the situation was still a bit defeating."

"Sure it is," Yanis replied. "Izzy and I seldom share our goals with anybody, and if we do we make sure they are people we know to be supportive of our efforts. This is very important, Billy. Sometimes people say things unintentionally that offer their doubtful thoughts to you. Don't allow their doubts to affect your thoughts nor try to sell them on yours. As you move forward in your career, I suspect your production levels will raise questions and be admired by many. Stay private with your goals and focus only on their achievement. The opinion of others is not important. In time, as people take note of your continued success, they will allow their production beliefs to evolve. Consistent success is the greatest way to teach — it's by example. People learn from high achievers because they are proof of great possibilities. Remember, it's best to privately set your goals and silently achieve them."

"I see your point," Billy responded. "But you speak as though I'm already this great and successful salesperson."

"Number one means number one," Yanis said. "Your position on the sales board is no fluke. In your industry, people admire high achievers. It's the nature of the business. If you dream of high achievements, see the dream clearly, believing without a doubt in its accomplishment. Then you can accept the high level of achievements into your life."

"How will I know when I reach that level?" Billy asked.

"You will know because you are living the dream and thinking about new ones. Remember what we said was at the top of 'Dream Mountain?' Now, Billy, let's say your next dream is something simple like drinking a hot cup of tea," Yanis replied. "When would you know you have aspired to the level of the dream?"

"When I could hold the cup in my hand, take a sip and begin dreaming of cookies to go with it." Billy answered quickly.

"That's exactly right," Yanis said proudly, just as Izzy walked through the barn door carrying a tray of refreshments.

"Tea and cookies for the hard working boat build-ers," she said.

Yanis quickly glanced at Billy. "You're getting pretty good at this stuff."

Billy burst out laughing, "I didn't do that."

"Of course you did. Be grateful. Were you dreaming of a cookie?"

"I guess she never has brought us cookies with our tea before." Billy shook his head enjoying her homemade treats.

They all three sat, admiring how different the boat looked with her new caprail. She was beginning to look fin-ished. The next few weeks would bring new stanchions, life-lines and paint completing her refit.

"Yanis," Izzy reminded, "you promised me many years ago that when you rebuilt her I could give her a proper name. While we were on our voyage you wouldn't let me change her mind in fear of attracting bad luck." With a smile she added, "I already know what her name is going to be."

"What?" Yanis and Billy both spoke up simultane-ously.

"I'm not telling. It's going to be a surprise," Izzy re-ported. "So you might as well not ask again."

"Well, I don't really remember saying that," Yanis playfully said, knowing he had. "But, if you say I did then I will stand by my word. But Izzy, don't name her something like Wavedancer or Sea Goddess, or something silly. It has to be something original, okay?"

"Oh, it will be original, I promise," she said, wiggling her eyebrows.

Yanis shook his head at Izzy. Sometimes she could really be a pistol.

"Whatever happened to Alexander?" Billy questioned out of the blue.

Izzy spoke up. "He passed only two months after our wedding."

Billy sighed, "I'm sorry. I bet that was tough."

"Well, I guess it was hard at the time. But Billy, that was sixty-some years ago. Alexander was getting up in years. And he was ready. He completed what he came to do."

"The stories you've been telling me makes it seem like yesterday," Billy replied.

"It does to me too," Izzy confirmed. "My grandfather was a wonderful man. If I recall, we all three sailed from Water Island to Mountain Island the day after Yanis proposed to me. I couldn't wait to tell my parents."

"I remember that," Yanis added. "Alexander and I caught a couple more bigheaded fish on the way over."

"Were you using Alexander's special reed lure?" Billy asked. "You know the one that wouldn't work."

They all three laughed at his comment, especially Yanis. "Of course," he said.

"I remember my parent's reaction when I introduced them to Yanis and told them the news of our marriage," Izzy said. "They were very happy for me, but cautious at the same time."

"I'd say they were pretty lucky I found my way to

your island in the first place, if you ask me," Yanis interjected quickly.

"I don't think you found the way, I think that boat of yours found it for you," Izzy returned playfully. "And besides, who asked you anyway?"

Yanis gave her a dejected expression.

"You were pretty cocky back then," she continued. "You were sure you could do anything any other man on the island could do."

"Was not cocky," Yanis rebutted with a prankish smile. "I was just really sure of myself, that's all."

"You remember the time the lobster men invited us to go spear fishing with them?" Izzy asked.

"You would remember the one time I had a bit of difficulty, wouldn't you?" returned Yanis.

"I remember the story exactly as it happened," she said. "You and I sailed out to the outer reef with two divers from the village. We anchored the boat in a patch of sand. Putting on flippers and masks, we quietly slipped into the water so we wouldn't alarm the fish. When you looked down and saw the reef below us, you exclaimed, 'that's a long way down.'"

"It was a long way down," Yanis confirmed with emotion, trying to save face. "It had to be at least fifty or fifty-five feet to the reef. That is a long way to free dive."

"I knew I couldn't make it down that deep," Izzy said. "So I paddled around on top and let the divers go down and make the harvest. I remember you made it about fifteen feet before you turned and came back to the top."

"My ears were hurting, that's why. And besides, it was more than fifteen feet," Yanis said matter-of-factly.

"You tried and tried to get deeper, but each time you had to return to the surface because of your ears," Izzy reminded him again in jest. "Then the other divers came to the surface and that was the final blow. They each had two huge lobsters impaled on their spears. That just about killed you, remember?" she said with a laugh.

"I was a bit embarrassed at that," Yanis agreed.

"But in fairness to you, you went out with the divers every day for the entire month prior to our wedding. And each day your dives got deeper and deeper. I remember the day you went diving with Alexander; he was so excited because you had the deepest dive, sixty feet. Remember, you shot the largest hogfish snapper Alexander had ever seen? Even the other two divers were impressed." Izzy stopped her story long enough for her and Billy to acknowledge Yanis' wide smile and stuck out chest.

Then she continued. "You know, Yanis, I think you inviting Alexander diving is the only thing that kept him on Mountain Island because when he was in the village, all he could ever talk about was going home to Water Island. Immediately after the wedding, he got his wish. The three of us sailed back to Water Island and your sailboat became our first home. We lived in the quiet anchorage at the base of the mountain, where Alexander could look down and see us from his hut anytime he felt lonely. Of course, we were always climbing the mountain to swim in the pool and be with him."

"So it was two months after you moved to the boat that Alexander passed?" Billy questioned Izzy.

"Yes, we lived in that peaceful lagoon for two months," Izzy confirmed. "Yanis would dive every couple of days for lobsters or snappers. Of course, we always shared everything with Alexander. The excitement he showed early on when we took him fresh fish seemed to gradually lesson. Alexander seemed to be failing, and for no apparent reason. When I questioned him about how he felt he would always say. 'Fine, Izzy, just fine. I'm just getting tired. You will know when it is my time to pass.' I never really knew how I was to know, but I trusted I would. Sometimes I think his watching us and seeing our love for each other made him feel even lonelier for my grandmother. I think he missed her so much, it may have hastened his passing."

"So, when he passed, how did you know?" Billy asked. "Or did you know?"

"Well, as I said, Alexander was really getting weak. His mind was clear, but he had no energy and even with my continual urging, he did nothing to strengthen himself. He had no more desires. That's when I figured his time was getting close. All we could do was watch him."

Billy shook his head. "What a great loss," he said. "Alexander was the last Kahuna."

"As far as we knew he was. But the Pacific Ocean is large and its islands are many, so one never really knows. One day toward the end of Alexander's life," Izzy continued without elaborating further about Billy's comment. "Yanis and I were sitting by the stream near the lagoon. I waded out into the stream and knelt down. I remember how cool the water felt that day. I saw a slight movement floating on the surface of the water toward me. Reaching down I held my hands open, a small yellow bird, a Golden Canary, floated into my palms. I picked it up and gently blew on it in an effort to help it dry. The poor little creature tried to roll over onto its stomach, but couldn't. It had ingested too much water. The little yellow bird stretched its wings and raised its head one last time gasping for air. Then it closed its eyes and died. Suddenly, I felt a quick shock shoot through my body. I knew immediately, I don't know how I knew, I just knew. 'Alexander, Alexander!' I screamed at Yanis. 'My grandfather is dying. We have to hurry.' Somehow, I knew the yellow bird was the sign my grandfather had promised."

"Did you make it to him in time?" Billy asked, leaning forward on the edge of his chair.

"We ran up the mountain as quickly as we could. When Yanis and I entered the clearing, Alexander was kneeling beside Grandmother's grave. He was slowly swaying back and forth. We knelt down beside him. I was on one side and Yanis on the other. Alexander asked if we could lie him down on his back. We helped him lie down.

"'Izzy,' he said. 'I have taught you for years the teachings of the old masters. You, my granddaughter, are now 'the keeper of the secret.' I have shared with you all I know. The teachings are yours to share. I have great appreciation for my time with you, my granddaughter. I will always love you very much.'

"'I love you too, Grandfather,' I told him through

tears. 'But how will I know who to share the teachings with?' I asked as he faded.

"'You needn't look for people to teach, they will look for you. You will know who they are in your heart because you will see the questions in their eyes,' he replied.

"I knelt down close to my grandfather and gently held his head to my chest. He closed his eyes and died in my arms. It was what he wanted."

"Wow, what a sad story," Billy said, looking toward the ground. "Was he buried there on the hillside next to your grandmother?"

"Yes, he was. I think the entire village came for his passing ceremony," Izzy answered. "It was only a few days later that Yanis and I said goodbye to my family and friends. We sailed away toward the setting sun."

"Alexander called you the 'keeper of the secret,' Billy said. "Is that true? Are you a Kahuna, like Alexander?"

"In my grandfather's eyes, I think I was," Izzy answered. "I didn't stay on the islands to continue in his path and be the Kahuna, I chose to leave with Yanis. The teachings he taught are similar to what I teach and practice today. The powers of the old Kahunas are available to all through the power of positive and directed thought. But Billy, even though this knowledge can benefit everyone, few people will take the time and effort to actually apply this wisdom to their lives."

"Why is that?" Billy asked. "How can you not want to utilize something so beneficial?"

"I think people are resistant to change," she responded. "It could be lots of reasons. You will find many people rooted in some level of comfort. There is a certain safety in numbers; security in the masses. There are many salespeople, some successful and some very successful. But there are very few who reach the highest levels of achievement—the big dreamers. It takes a clear desire and a lot of courage to stand out from the crowd to seek a dream, others cannot yet see. But holding fast to your course, you can reach the higher levels you seek. And when you do, a new and special gift will unfold."

"What gift is that?" Billy asked.

"The vision of your next dream," she replied. "It's our nature, Billy. Accomplishing one desire clears the pathway for the new desire to be realized."

"I don't know about that," Billy replied. "If I work real hard and stay focused on my goals, when I finally achieve them, I'm sure I'll set back and enjoy the achievement for a while. I don't think I'd immediately come up with another goal and start all over again."

Izzy smiled at Billy's comment. "Maybe," she said.

Even though Billy understood what Izzy was saying, he still didn't think it was true in his case. *This is a good time to change the subject*, he thought.

"Where did you go from Water Island?" he questioned.

"We sailed to many places over the next four years," she returned. We sailed to Tahiti, Tonga, New Zealand, Australia, through the Indian Ocean down to South Africa, then north and west into the Caribbean Ocean, stopping briefly at the island of Utilla, before finally making landfall in America."

"You two have sure had an adventurous life," Billy replied, shaking his head slowly. "It kind of makes my normal life seem pretty mundane. You said you stopped briefly at the island of Utilla; where is that?

"Utilla is a very small island off the north coast of Honduras. It is one of the bay islands in the Honduran archipelago."

"I know where that is," Billy excitedly replied. "Dana and I met another couple about six or seven months ago who were sailing the world aboard their sailboat. We met them in Roatan, an island off the north coast of Honduras. It's part of the same island chain. I remember looking at the beautiful boat they sailed in on and anchored in the sheltered lagoon where we sat having lunch. I remember how the adventurous life our friends described had such a profound impression on me. I also remember looking at Dana and telling her 'someday, just maybe that could be us.'"

"Sounds like a dream seed was planted to me," Izzy said softly.

Billy and Yanis smiled at each other and decided to take the rest of the day off from boat building. Yanis was tired and Billy anxious to get to the office and begin his phone calls for next week's new plan. Last night's success provided the six referrals he needed to fill his lunch dates.

9

EXPECTANCY

It's when you know the time is now
That fear and doubt will flee,
Expectancy and faith is how
Your eyes will come to see.

Billy decided to give his new plan a two-part possibility for success. If he kept evening appointments on Monday, Wednesday and Friday, and luncheon appointments on Tuesday and Thursday, it would allow the most versatility for his customers. At this point, he barely had ten referral names, so if one or more couldn't make the luncheon, Billy would have to scramble to fill the spots. It would be a good opportunity for him to invite one of his past customers to attend the luncheon, kind of as a 'thank you.'

Billy started calling his list of referrals. For the most part, his plan was working. The people he spoke with did find a free lunch inviting. If they couldn't make Tuesday, he offered Thursday. If neither of the luncheons worked, he offered the evening slots. His week was filling nicely, but he ran out of names. Billy could see how after he had a full week of appointments, he should have enough referrals to completely fill the next week's schedule. But the first week he would have to fill the luncheons with past customers, hoping they would bring friends.

With his work done, Billy couldn't wait to call Dana and relay the story Izzy shared with him about her adventures with Yanis, their wedding and Alexander's passing. Even though Dana wasn't physically in Colorado with Billy, she was very much involved emotionally in what he was learning from the Bartons'. She could see her life changing along with his. With Billy's daily calls relaying success, Dana's excitement grew quickly. She was soon in the mode of creating new dreams of their life in Colorado. She became more expectant of Billy's regular successful appointments. She expected him to call every day and give her more good news. And the more she expected it, the more it seemed to happen. They were both learning rapidly how this process worked. Their expectancy and appreciation was becoming natural. It was now habit.

The following week was a busy one for Billy. Because of his luncheon appointments, he was only able to help Yanis a few hours Monday, Wednesday and Friday. Yanis and Billy spent their limited time together working on the second caprail and talked very little. By Friday afternoon, the rail was finished. The following week they planned to tape and mask all the wood and port lights, preparing the boat for the painter who was scheduled to paint the next week. The painter said he needed the entire week to apply all the coats of paint necessary to give the boat the look and sheen Yanis wanted.

This week had not only been successful in their completing of the caprail, but for Billy personally also. He received the production award and the bonus check that had been promised. He found he wasn't nearly as embarrassed with the attention as he thought he might be. He was actually beginning to like it. And his new luncheon appointments were proving very successful. He discovered having past customers present at the luncheons provided confirmation of their satisfaction in his product. It added real validity to Billy's presentation. It made his job much easier.

Billy ended on Friday evening with a total weekly production of twenty-six sales. He added the twenty-three from the first week, giving him a total of forty-nine. One hundred sales didn't seem so far away. Billy could see it happening. The planner was working. Smiling, Billy called Dana to share his excitement with her.

Billy only had one thing in his planner for Saturday. He needed to call all the referrals he'd collected during the week to try to fill next week's schedule. It had been a good week for referrals thus he was certain he would have enough names. He put the calling off until the afternoon so he could visit the Bartons in the morning.

Yanis was moving slowly when Billy got to the farm. The extra effort he put out to finish the caprail with Billy had taxed his energy. He slept beyond the six a.m. coffee-pot timer. Izzy moved around the house quietly, letting her husband sleep. It was almost eight o'clock when Yanis crawled out of bed.

Having just picked up his first cup of coffee, he sat down on the porch swing with Goose and Izzy.

"Missed the sunrise," she said smiling. "I can't remember the last time you did that."

"Yes," Yanis said. "I just feel kind of worn out."

"Maybe you should let Billy tape and mask the wood on the boat," she suggested. "He would love to do it and you don't need to be climbing around the scaffolding all day."

"Maybe you're right," he agreed. "Don't know if he's coming today or not. He left in a hurry yesterday to get to his appointments."

"That boy sure is doing well, isn't he?" Izzy commented. "We sure have become attached to him in a short period of time."

"I know, it's like he's been in our lives for years, but it's only been two weeks," Yanis replied. "We both knew he would do well. We saw it in him. I really do like Billy. Everything he touches seems to be working for him. He sure was excited yesterday, telling us about his success with his luncheon appointments. He's pretty proud of his first-class ticket to you know what?"

"Yes, I do," she agreed, "the 'Prosperity Train,' and it's rolling again."

Goose heard the car approaching and just raised her head. She knew it was Billy by the sound of his car engine.

Billy stopped the car and got out.

"Come and have a seat," Izzy told him. "We were just wondering if you were coming today. I have fresh coffee." She went to get him a cup.

"Thank you," Billy replied. "I guess I don't really know why I came by this morning. Maybe it's just becoming habit or something?"

"I don't think it's habit, Billy," Izzy said. "I think you are feeling things that direct your actions. With your wife and children not here, it is natural that you follow your feelings to the closest thing to family. That would be Yanis and me. Similar energy vibrations attract, remember. You will find that through life, many friends come and go. Those friends whose attitudes, characteristics and beliefs change with yours remain close or even get closer. Those friends who either don't change in the direction you change or just remain unchanged, move into different levels of friendship. That doesn't mean they are no longer friends; they're no longer intimate friends. Maybe they are a bit more distant. Some of the friends you have today might have been friends you've had for years and years. But more often than not, the closest friends you have are the friends moving in the same direction that life is leading you. Similar energy vibrations will always attract in their likeness.

"When you are aware of this, you will find it interesting how often people pass through your life. What may appear as a happenstance meeting the first time you meet someone may become a close friend the second or third time your paths cross. Now the friendship grows strong very quickly. It is because either you or your friend grows to mirror a similar energy level as the other."

"I think I see how that could be the case," Billy agreed. "It makes sense."

"What would you like to do today?" Yanis asked Billy.

"Well, I know next week is going to be pretty busy for me at work with my new sales presentations," Billy replied. "Maybe we should do some of next week's boat chores today. I don't have to be anywhere until late this afternoon, so we have quite a while."

Izzy interjected quickly, "Yanis and I were talking about this earlier. He should stay off the scaffoldings for a while. He's not feeling very strong today. He can sit in the chair and instruct you on how to mask and tape."

"That sounds perfect to me," Billy agreed. "Who knows, if you lean that chair of yours up against the wall, you may even fall asleep."

Yanis smiled shaking his head at Billy's remark. "You'll never let me live that one down, will you?"

After they finished their coffee, Yanis explained what had to be done on the boat and showed Billy where the supplies were. Then he moved his chair against the wall and sat down to watch Billy work.

Taping and masking the new caprails and all the port lights would be easy, but it was time-consuming tearing all the small pieces of tape used to create the curve around the rounded surfaces. But, by lunchtime his perseverance paid off; the chore was completed.

Billy, who had been working on the opposite side of the boat for the last hour, was out of sight from Yanis. When he stuck his head up to declare the job complete, he noticed Yanis leaning against the wall. His prediction had been correct. The old man was sound asleep.

Billy quietly climbed down from the deck of the boat. Slowly, he made his way out of the barn. From the kitchen window, Izzy saw him coming as she made sandwiches for lunch.

"Where is Yanis?" she questioned, meeting him at the front door.

"He's sleeping," he answered. "I quietly left the barn so I wouldn't wake him."

"I appreciate that, Billy," she said. "He does need his rest. He has sure slowed down this past year. Though, I have to admit since you showed up I have seen a marked difference in his attitude. It seemed to drive him on to complete the boat. You have been very good for Yanis. I appreciate you being our friend."

Billy bowed his head slightly as he saw the sincerity in Izzy's eyes. It was hard for him to believe she was thanking him for his friendship when he felt such gratitude for their friendship. He loved Izzy and Yanis; he loved them like they were his own family. To Billy, in his heart, they were.

"I probably should be getting back to town," Billy said. "I've got some calls to make. Everything is done in preparation of the painter."

"Wonderful, Billy," she returned. "We so appreciate your help. Take your sandwich for the road. I'll go sit beside Yanis until he wakes. I like to keep him company when he falls asleep in his chair like this." Izzy stepped off the porch and Goose followed her into the barn.

Billy smiled at Izzy; she was a special woman.

10

ACCEPTANCE

Hold very clear your dream in thought
And know that this is how,
To build the pathway dreams are brought
Into your here and now.

Billy's referral list was growing. Everyone he called was interested in hearing his presentation. He now needed to expand his luncheon appointments to three days a week to make room for everyone who wanted to attend.

The week progressed very well and by Tuesday evening, Billy had eighteen more sales. His total was sixty-seven, only three short of his original goal of seventy he had with Dana. He was elated with his success. He called Dana with the news.

"You're going to make it this week," she said. "I just know it."

"Plan to come home this weekend," Billy said with excitement.

"Remember, tomorrow we are going to the beach

with my parents. We will be away for two days. Back late Thursday night. We won't be able to talk until then. I have my fingers crossed. Call me Friday morning, okay?"

Billy promised and told Dana, "Goodnight." He had his second luncheon meeting scheduled for the following day, plus two appointments that evening. When Billy went to bed, he slept well knowing his plan was working. He could feel the joy of his success and his goal within his grasp.

Thursday morning arrived and Billy went into the office to turn in fourteen more sales contracts from the previous day. One of his appointments the evening before had bought two. Billy's total was now eighty-one. He couldn't wait to tell Dana it was time to buy their return airplane tickets.

Thursday's luncheon produced eighteen more sales agreements. He was on cloud nine.

It's almost too much, he thought. *From the pain of loss I felt a few days ago to the complete joy I feel now. From a struggling career to record-setting sales performances in such a short time is mind boggling. This 'Prosperity Train' is moving fast for the McCoy family.* He smiled at his thought. He knew he wouldn't want it any other way. He drove back to the office to turn in the new sales agreements. As he drove, it dawned on him that he had beaten his sales record and now the company had another new weekly record. *Another thousand dollars*, he thought.

The following day, Billy planned to preview apartments to have a list of the best for Dana to see when she returned.

That night as Billy sat at home, he reflected back on

three weeks of performance. The huge goal he and Dana agreed upon didn't seem so huge anymore.

Friday morning, Billy awoke at six a.m. and called his wife while he still lay in bed.

"Dana," he said, certain he was awakening her. "What do you think happened this week?"

"Billy, we haven't talked since Tuesday night. You were getting close to our goal. I know what you're going to say. You made it, didn't you? Tell me you made the goal." she exclaimed with anticipation.

"We are talking big numbers," he returned. "Really big numbers."

"Well, tell me."

"Ninety-nine," he said.

"We'll be on a plane in two days," she screamed without any hesitation. "I knew you could do it, Billy. I just knew you could. But, you didn't just do it, you really did it. Ninety-nine is four times the monthly record for the company, and you did it in three weeks. You have another week to go this month."

"Dana," Billy said on a serious note. "I've been thinking about something. With all the referrals I have from this week, I'll have to have three luncheons again next week. I bet I could sell another fifty if I try. That will give us one hundred and forty-nine for the four-week period. And that's if I don't sell any this evening. It will be a busy week between work and us moving again. I will spend most of today previewing apartments for us. I'll pick the top possibilities and you can make the final choice when you arrive. We can move between my appointments. It will give us an entire year's savings account cushion. What do you think?"

"Go for it," she quickly agreed. "Go for it. I'll buy the plane tickets today. Saturday we say our goodbyes and pack. Sunday we are coming home."

As Billy hung up the phone, he thought about his achievement and felt a rush of pure bliss and contentment. Accomplishing this level of performance was such a benefit to his family. It opened doors he never realized were there. One of the most important was what he was able to focus on now. He now always thought of successful presentations. He never thought of the money he needed for day-to-day living expenses. The more he focused on his successful career, the more successful ideas flowed. Just looking beyond his company's traditional marketing process, as Yanis suggested, stimulated the creativity necessary to realize a new sales process. Now, by using that process, his goal of seventy sales was complete.

He flashed on Jack's comment while in Roatan. "Hold fast to your dreams. It's in their achievement life's greatest contentment is found." Billy could see that now. He agreed.

Billy's mind couldn't let go of the possibility of selling one hundred and fifty in one month. After all, reaching his first goal of seventy sales proved to be easy. One hundred fifty now seemed very reachable. Billy couldn't wait to share this new goal with Yanis and Izzy. They would be so proud of him. Billy remembered Izzy's comment earlier; she had said, 'When you reach a goal, the gift of another will appear.'

Billy had been convinced that he wouldn't jump right into pursuit of another goal. He thought he would sit back and enjoy his accomplishment. Billy now remembered her sweet smile. He knew she was correct. He was already pushing forward to the next level.

Having been so busy all week, Billy had only talked with Izzy a couple of times by phone. She said Yanis was still moving very slowly. "Come by when you can," she said to Billy. "We would like that."

As the sun rose Saturday, he was up early. The first thing on his list was breakfast. So off he drove to his favorite diner. Billy ordered what he called his 'successful salesperson breakfast.'

After breakfast, Billy stopped at the office for more forms. He entered the large central office only to run into the two salespeople who voiced their doubt about his production expectations earlier.

Funny, Billy thought. *I never thought of their comments again after speaking to Yanis and Izzy about them.*

The two approached Billy. "Ninety-nine sales agreements in three weeks," the first one said. "That is more than anyone in this office could even imagine. I don't know how you did it, Billy, but great job. It's obvious it's not just luck." The men took turns shaking his hand.

"Thank you," Billy said humbly. "It means a lot to me for you to say that." Respect from one's peers is very important, and Billy sure respected the two of them.

Before leaving the office, Billy turned in another sales agreement from the night before, making his total sales for the month an even one hundred.

That day as he drove down the driveway toward the Barton's house, Billy noticed the ears of corn hanging out from the stalk. *They look fat and ripe,* he thought. *It's nearly harvest time.*

He parked at the house in his normal spot. As he got out of his car, he saw Yanis sitting in the swing.

"Did you see the sunrise this morning?" Billy asked.

"No, Billy, I didn't," he replied. "I missed it again."

That concerned Billy.

Izzy stepped out of the house as cheerful as ever. "Hey, Billy, want some coffee?"

"I would love some," he returned. "It looks to me like the corn is getting ripe."

"As a matter of fact, the corn in the garden needs to be picked today," she responded. "Would you like some corn to take home?"

"Well, I guess I might as well because I have special news today," Billy returned.

"And what might that be?" Izzy asked.

"Dana and the kids are coming home tomorrow," he answered quickly. "I hit and zoomed right past my goal of seventy." Billy proudly strutted around comically.

"That is wonderful, Billy," Izzy and Yanis said together, both clapping their hands in congratulation. "We are so proud of you."

"Bring your coffee," Yanis said, standing slowly. "Izzy, come with us."

Billy and Izzy followed him as he walked very slowly

toward the garden. He stepped up to the first stalk of corn.

"Billy, come pick this ear of corn and tell me exactly what you are doing," Yanis instructed.

Billy did what Yanis asked. He picked the ear of corn and began to shuck it.

"I know the answer is not just I am picking an ear of corn — that would be far too easy," Billy responded. "So I suppose the correct answer to your questions is this: I am in acceptance of the dream of an ear of corn."

Yanis smiled broadly at Billy's answer. And so did Izzy, then they both said together, "We hear that 'Prosperity Train,' Billy, but it's not coming any longer, the train is already here, and you have a first-class ticket. No need ever to have any more doubt in the process. Whether your goal is an ear of corn or record-breaking sales, the knowledge gained from your experience can never be lost."

"Let's pick some corn and other veggies for your family. They'll be hungry when they get here. We still expect you to come and visit as often as you can. Now you can bring your family with you. Your family is our family. Promise us that, okay?"

Billy promised and they went to work in the garden picking vegetables not only for his family, but for the homeless as well. Yanis tired quickly and sat in the shade beside the tall corn stalks as Izzy and Billy finished picking the vegetables.

Billy left for town. He dropped some of the veggies off at his friend's house and took the rest to the shelter. Now it was time to finish making the referral calls and filling next week's schedule.

He really wanted this next week of sales to be special. By six p.m., he had made his calls. But Billy knew how beneficial inviting past customers to his luncheons had been, so he decided to do it again. Besides, he enjoyed the continued contact.

That night Billy was happy to be able to write a check to his friend for rent and the use of his garage for storage. His friend didn't want to accept it, but Billy insisted.

"I think a camping trip is in order," Billy told Dana when they spoke that evening. "When we get moved into our new apartment, we should take a little vacation."

"Camping would be wonderful. I know the kids would love it," she agreed. "Where do you think we should go?"

"Someplace in the back country where there are no phones," he responded. "We shouldn't tell anyone where we're going either — agreed?"

"Most definitely," she said. "Maybe we should make it a full two weeks, if you don't think that will bother your work schedule too much. You deserve a break."

"Dana," Billy replied, "with this new appointment format, I don't think it will have much effect at all. I will just have two weeks less next month to work. But, we are already way ahead of schedule. Dana, I love you. I'll see you tomorrow at the airport."

They hung up and Billy relaxed, content with his life. The next day he would get his family back. It would be another good day for Billy McCoy.

Sunday, Dana and the kids arrived midmorning. They spent a couple of hours that afternoon looking at the apartments Billy had picked as options. After choosing one they agreed on, everything was in order to start their move.

Monday morning they moved the larger furniture, and then in the afternoon they moved most of the boxes before Billy left for his evening appointments.

Tuesday morning before his luncheon appointment, they finished hauling everything to their new apartment. All was going as planned. By Tuesday evening, Dana was busy putting it all in place.

Tuesday night, Billy's sales totaled seventeen for the week. He was on track.

"Tomorrow is Wednesday," Dana reminded him. "It's school registration, and it starts early." Registering his son in kindergarten was a big deal and Billy wanted to be there. He arranged his luncheon appointment for after the school registration.

Wednesday's sales luncheon again proved very successful. When it was finished, Billy was only nineteen short of his goal. With one more luncheon and a couple of evening appointments left, he had a real shot at reaching his goal of one hundred fifty.

With his family back, Billy's life sure became much busier. He didn't mind at all, but here another week came and went and he didn't have time to visit Yanis and Izzy. He would call them on Saturday morning before he and the family left for their camping trip. Once they returned from the trip, things would settle down. He was sure of it. He had to get his family out to meet his new friends.

Friday evening as Billy walked out of his last appointment, the magnitude of his accomplishment had not registered yet. There were things going on with his manager and the home office that Billy wasn't aware of. The idea that a new salesperson could come in and demolish a fifteen-year-old sales record by systematically quadrupling it was something every manager in the company wanted an explanation for. But that explanation and goal-setting process was something Billy had already learned to keep to himself cautiously. Further explanation would have to wait for two weeks. He and his family were going camping.

Saturday morning came. Billy quickly turned in his last two days of sales agreements, giving him a grand total of one hundred fifty-one for the month. He slipped out of the office before anyone else could see him. He called Izzy and Yanis, explaining he was taking his family camping for two weeks. He would see them immediately when he returned.

Izzy told him Yanis seemed a bit weaker, but he sure got excited when he finally saw his sailboat painted. "She is beautiful, Billy. The painter is helping install the hardware. Yanis wants you to come by the minute you return from camping. You have to see the boat and we want to meet your family."

Billy agreed. With the car loaded, they all piled in and off they went. Yellowstone National Park in northwestern Wyoming was their destination. The station wagon came in handy. They put the tent, camp stove, and the other camping necessities in the rear. The kids got the back seat to themselves, while Billy drove with Dana at his side.

It was a long day's drive but they made it. Finding the most remote campsite available, Billy and Dana decided to pitch camp and settle in. Everything was perfect, even down to the fishing stream alongside the campsite.

In Billy's mind, he was in heaven. He had money in the bank, his family at his side, and a career that was bursting at the seams. It was everything he had dreamed of. The only thing he would change is the slight gnawing inside he felt about not seeing Yanis and Izzy before he left. He knew they understood, but it didn't eliminate his feelings. He loved them so much. When their vacation was over, they would go see them. He couldn't wait for his family to meet his new friends.

By the end of the first week Billy was on vacation, Yanis and the painter finished installing all the hardware on the deck of the boat. Actually, the painter did all the work. Yanis was too weak even to climb onto the deck. He seemed to get weaker day by day. Izzy was getting very concerned, but Yanis kept telling her he was fine, just a little tired.

With the paint job finished, it was time for the name to be painted across the stern. Yanis was anxious to see what Izzy had chosen. "Are you ready to give us the name?" he asked Izzy. "Today is the day."

"No, it's still a secret," she replied. "I want you to see it after it's painted. I want it to be in bright gold letters, okay?"

"Agreed," Yanis said, nodding his head at his wife's prankish behavior. Tired, Yanis sat down in one of the chairs.

All he wanted to do was admire the beautiful old boat. He had completed his promise to this old girl. She was as good as new. With her new name, she would have a new life. She would outlive Yanis, and he knew that. After all, he owed his life to the sailboat — she deserved anything Yanis could do for her.

Izzy told the painter the name she wanted painted across the stern of the boat.

An hour later, she stood back and took the first look. She smiled. It was perfect.

Izzy helped her husband to his feet. She could see he was even weaker than earlier that day. She took both chairs and followed Yanis to the stern of the boat. She placed the chairs at just the right angle to view the entire side of the hull and the stern of the boat at the same time.

Now, as Yanis turned and sat down, he looked toward his faithful friend. He saw her new name for the first time. The name Izzy chose brought tears to his eyes. He gave his wife the nod of approval. Both Yanis and Izzy's dream was now complete. His sixty-four-year-old promise to restore his old boat was accomplished, and Izzy finally had given her a proper name.

Yanis took his wife's hand and lightly squeezed.

"Everything I have ever dreamed of in this life has come to pass," he told her. "From big dreams like our love, a beautiful family and great success to small dreams that might seem insignificant to some, like rebuilding an old sailboat. I am content, Izzy. I am very content. I know how Alexander felt many years ago. I am old and weak and I feel my time is very near. Sitting beside me are two of the most beautiful things in my life. I could ask for nothing more. Izzy, I feel very weak." He leaned forward against his wife as she now knelt beside him.

Izzy held her husband's head close to her chest. Her eyes filled with tears as she thought, *The old man has just been waiting for the completion of this old sailboat.* She saw that and knew that was what he wanted.

"Yanis, my life has also been as complete and full as yours. I do not choose to continue without you. If you choose to leave, I choose to follow. I will see you very soon, my dear," she whispered softly. The painter helped Izzy get Yanis into the house and gently lay him down on the couch. He closed his eyes and slept.

Yanis Barton passed away that evening with his wife by his side.

He didn't want a big ceremony. However, that desire proved impossible to keep from happening. His long and philanthropic life had affected so many people. Thousands of friends and business associates wanted to express their condolences to his family.

Izzy took the whole process in stride. Certainly, she mourned her late husband's passing and missed him dearly, but she knew their separation was only temporary.

Her son Jack and his wife Lucy flew in from their sailboat in the Caribbean. They came from Guatemala City the day after Yanis passed. The grandchildren arrived and everyone pitched in to help Izzy with all the arrangements. It made things much easier. As the number desiring to attend the ceremony grew and grew, Izzy held to her intention. She wanted to be available personally to every single person in attendance. She knew how much they all loved her late husband. She wanted to honor their feelings.

But, one thing she was immensely saddened by was the fact nobody, not even Billy's office, knew of his whereabouts. He and Dana had left telling no one where they were going.

But, saddened as she was, Izzy didn't mind. She knew how much Billy missed his family. This was their time to re-bond with each other. They would be back soon enough.

By the end of the ceremony, things began to settle down a bit. The following week, Jack and Izzy went through all the legal paperwork to sort out Yanis' estate. It went smoothly because he was very organized.

As the week wore on, Izzy started to become lethargic. She knew this would happen and was prepared for it. To Izzy, the purpose of continuing her life seemed pointless without Yanis. She loved her family very much, but she was so connected to her husband her own will to continue living had waned. She knew in her heart her own time to pass was quickly coming.

Somehow, Jack also knew. He saw how strong she was for all the people at the ceremony. But once she knew everything was in order, Izzy collapsed. They took her to the emergency room at the local hospital. The doctors could find nothing wrong physically. They assumed it must be stress. They put her in the Intensive Care Unit because her vital signs kept dropping for no apparent reason. Izzy was soon comatose. She seemed to be hanging on for something, but no one knew what.

On Saturday, exactly two weeks after Billy and Dana left with the kids, they packed up their gear and started for home.

Billy still felt anxious about not having seen the Bartons before he left. He wasn't able to put his finger on why, but Yanis and Izzy kept coming up in his thoughts. There were no phones where they were camped, so Billy just kept telling himself things were alright and he would check on them when they got home.

It was after midnight when the McCoys finally got to their apartment. They entered the house and the first message Billy listened to on the phone made him turn white. He broke down in tears.

The message said that Yanis Barton had passed away last week. His son, Jack Barton, was in town and needed Billy to get in touch with him as soon as he could.

"He died, Dana, Yanis died," Billy told her between the tears. "I knew something was up and I didn't act on it. I didn't get to say goodbye to the greatest man I ever met. He has changed my life forever. I didn't pay attention when I knew I needed to see him."

Billy and Dana lay awake all night. Billy mourned his cherished friend and mentor. He cried and cried, not believing he had so quickly lost Yanis, a friend who had given him and his family so very, very much.

The following morning, as early as Billy thought appropriate, he called Jack Barton.

"Hello," Jack answered, "Jack Barton here."

"This is Billy McCoy," Billy said. "I got your message. How can I help?"

"I am sorry we weren't able to reach you for the passing ceremony, Billy. We tried but no one knew where you were. My family and I are in town and would like to meet you and your family at the farm, if we could. You seem to have captured my parent's hearts. You are very special to them and, therefore, you are very special to me."

"Jack," Billy responded in a very shaky voice. "They have been the most wonderful people I have ever known. How is Izzy holding up?"

Jack sadly smiled when Billy called his mother Izzy. He knew then they had told Billy the story.

"My mother is not well. We put her in the hospital several days ago," he replied. "She is not expected to live much longer."

Billy felt another shockwave hit his body. "Jack, I would love to come by the farm, but first I have to go by the hospital," Billy returned. "Why don't we meet you in about two hours at your parent's farm?"

"Two hours would be fine," Jack answered. "But, Billy, she is in a coma."

"I understand," Billy said.

Billy, his wife and his kids quickly left to go see Izzy. Hospital rules would not allow the kids into the ICU, so Billy and Dana left them in the waiting room.

As they entered Izzy's room, Billy stepped to her side. A nurse came in and told them Izzy appeared to be rest-ing quietly, but in her condition, she probably wouldn't realize they were even in the room.

Billy thanked the nurse. Lifting Izzy's hand, he softly said, "Izzy Barton," before he could get the rest of the sentence out tears flowed down his face. "I am so sorry I wasn't here for you and Yanis. I am here now. Billy looked at Dana as a big sob took his composure. Dana wrapped her arm around his shoulder. "I want to introduce you to my wife, Dana," he said between sobs. I know you know we are here. We cannot stay long. We have to leave so you can rest. I will come back every day until you wake up, I promise."

Moments later, Billy and Dana left the room. Dana never said a word. She was caught up in her husband's emotion. She had never seen him like that. Her husband had changed somehow.

Billy drove the family to the Barton farm. As they parked in front of the house, Jack and Lucy stepped out onto the front porch.

Goose was lying under the porch for the first time since Billy had been coming to the farm. She seemed scared. Maybe a little lost. But the minute Billy stepped out of the car, Goose came quickly crawling out from under the porch and ran to Billy's side. Billy knelt down and held the old dog's head in his hands.

"It'll be okay, Goose," he said. "Sometimes things come at dogs the same as they do at people. Everything will be fine."

Billy's kids reached out and petted the old dog. Goose liked the attention.

As Billy and Dana looked up at Jack and Lucy, they both stopped dead in their tracks.

"Jack?" Billy said questioning. "Jack from Roatan?"

Jack and Lucy's reaction was the same. All four stood on the porch in complete shock at the turn of events that lead their lives together again.

Billy immediately remembered Izzy's comment two weeks earlier when she said, "Friends often drift apart only to return again later in life when energy vibrations grow closer. Take notice," she had told Billy.

Billy did take notice and realized what was happening.

"Jack," Billy said again, trying his hardest to stay composed. "I am so very sorry for your father's passing. He was such a special person in my life. He and your mother took it upon themselves to change my life, and you cannot believe how much they succeeded. I never really knew why, but I will always cherish their friendship and the help they gave me."

"I appreciate your comments, Billy. I do know how much they can change people's lives. My parents thought you were very special, yourself. My mother spoke of you constantly when we arrived. I appreciate the help you have given them over these past few weeks. I know how much they loved you, Billy," Jack continued on a less emotional note. "We had the reading of my father's will the other day. I have something I need to show you, if you have a moment."

"Sure," Billy said, following Jack as he walked to the

barn. Lucy and Dana followed their husbands.

As soon as they entered the barn door, Billy saw it. The finished and perfect H-28 sailboat sat proud and pretty for all to see. Billy stood at her starboard side in complete admiration.

"Billy," Jack said, pointing toward the sailboat. "My father left her to you. He said you loved her as much as he did."

Billy was motionless for a full three minutes, not saying a word. He walked closer, admiring the perfect paint job. She was the most beautiful sailboat he had ever seen in his life. The light beige hull had a depth to its sheen like looking into water. The caprail was varnished to perfection. The stainless steel hardware reflected like a mirror.

Billy slowly walked beside her hull, running his finger along her dark blue cove stripe.

Not one imperfection, he thought. As he reached the bow of the boat, he began the same slow walking process down the opposite side. Everything seemed perfect. When he reached the stern of the boat, Billy remembered Izzy promising to give her a new name. He wanted to surprise himself, so he walked ten feet behind her stern with his eyes closed. His brief thought of Izzy made him sad. He knew she was so weak. He pictured her alone in her hospital bed. His mind was focused on Izzy as he opened his eyes to look at the name she had chosen for the boat.

There it was. Across the stern of his first sailboat were the brilliant, golden letters, *Yellow Bird.*

"*Yellow Bird,*" Billy exclaimed! He raced to where

Dana was standing. "Hurry, Dana, grab the kids. Izzy is dying. That is her sign to me. I know it is. Come on, we have to hurry." Billy gave no further explanation.

Jack and Lucy weren't sure what he meant, but followed anyway.

The traffic was heavy and slowed them down a little, but somehow Billy and Dana still made good time to the hospital. Jack and Lucy weren't so lucky.

Billy and Dana rushed to Izzy's room and quickly stepped to her side.

Billy gently held her hand. "Izzy, we are here," he said softly.

Izzy's eyes opened ever so slightly. "You must have seen *Yellow Bird*," she said.

Billy nodded. "I knew immediately," he said. "We came as quickly as we could."

Izzy looked at Dana, "I am pleased to meet you, Dana," she whispered, letting them both know she was aware of their earlier visit. "Billy, in *Yellow Bird's* navigation desk is Alexander's crocodile backpack. Inside is an envelope that contains the teachings of Alexander," she said in a voice you could barely hear. "The original teachings were passed down by the use of symbols and words coded with hidden meanings. I have translated the symbols and coded words. I have written the steps as Yanis and I understood them and shared with you. Do the same with whomever you choose. They are yours to pass on. I love you and wish you well."

"Wait, Izzy, how will I know who to share them with," Billy asked, quickly fighting back his tears.

"When you are ready to share them, you will know and they will know. There are many who want to learn. Share with all who seek. You will see the questions in their eyes. The world is ready for this information."

It was then that Jack and Lucy entered the room. Jack stepped to the other side of his mother's bed. Taking her other hand in his, he smiled down at Izzy. "We are here."

Izzy Barton squeezed both men's hands and smiled. "My life is complete," she said. She closed her eyes and passed.

Another death in the Barton family so close to the first had the entire city buzzing. It was no surprise that more people turned out for Izzy's passing then for Yanis'.

By the end of the week, Billy, Dana, Jack and Lucy were exhausted. But, just as Izzy had, they stayed and spoke with everyone who came to give their respect.

By the following weekend, Billy and Dana were starting to get their lives back to normal.

Jack and Lucy stayed on at the farm to get the harvest in.

Billy tried to get his mind back into work while contacting his referrals of almost four weeks prior. As he worked, he felt gratitude and admiration for his mentors, Yanis and Izzy. They gave him the start he dreamed of. He knew the rest was up to him.

With only one week left in the month, Billy set his goal at fifty. Next month he knew would be different. He would go for another record.

Maybe, he thought, *two hundred sales were in order.*

Now, that number didn't sound too difficult. He could hear Yanis' words in his mind, "Set your goals equal to or greater than your best production." He smiled to himself.

Throughout the following month, Billy was at the farm every spare minute he had. He couldn't seem to stay away from *Yellow Bird*. It was as if *Yellow Bird* had now become his connection to Yanis and Izzy.

Finally, one day Jack asked him. "Billy, why don't we put her in the lake, down in Pueblo? The lake is plenty large enough to learn how to sail. Lucy and I will be here for at least another month. We would love to teach you guys how to sail this beautiful little boat. What do you think?"

"Why, I think it is a great idea," Billy said with excitement. "What an opportunity. We could learn from the pros."

The following Sunday, *Yellow Bird* was officially launched under the proud ownership of Billy and Dana Mc-Coy.

Jack and Lucy happily toasted the launch with a bottle of champagne. They all spent the day sailing the lake from one end to the other. Billy and Dana continued to practice the correct terminology and sailor's jargon. It took awhile, but they slowly picked it up. Sailing the wonderful little sailboat was a thrill. Everyone loved it, even the kids.

On the next to the last day of the month, Billy was tallying his sales. Fifty-six the first week, fifty-three the second week, forty-three the third week and forty-four the fourth left Billy four behind his goal of two hundred.

It was late Friday night. Saturday was D-day — the

month would be over. Maybe he could call the next morning and set some last-minute presentations. He had to try something. He couldn't just give up — he was so close.

Before he could make the calls to arrange the appointments, his phone rang. It was Jack.

"Billy," something has come across my desk concerning you that we have to deal with tomorrow, if possible. Lucy and I have to leave and return to Guatemala on Sunday. Is there any chance of meeting with you tomorrow morning?"

"Of course," Billy said without hesitation, knowing this would probably keep him from having the time to set and give more presentations, but that was secondary to his friends. Billy was thankful for his tremendously successful month he'd already had. There was always next month. And besides, Billy had another new idea that just might take his sales performance to the next level.

Saturday morning, Billy and Dana took the kids to the farm. On the way Billy stopped at the first service station they passed for gas. After filling his fuel tank, he stepped inside to pay the cashier. He pulled out his wallet to get a credit card. There it was. His Magic Moment Goal folded and stuck in the corner of his wallet. He had forgotten about it with all that had been going on. He took it out and read the number written in the box. He was short, substantially short. But when he wrote the goal, he hadn't counted on a two-week vacation and the death of his mentors. He lost three weeks of production. It was not only the last day of the month, but was also the last day to achieve his Magic Moment Goal. It was the last day of the ninety-day performance period that he set with Yanis. He smiled to himself, realizing that even with the three weeks he hadn't worked he still achieved his three-month goal of three hundred sales. *That's okay*, he thought, momentarily disappointed about the Magic Moment Goal. His mind shifted immediately as he remembered and appreciated what he had already accomplished.

"Billy, the Magic Moment Goals are just as important as the others." Yanis had told him. "But we'll talk about that more in ninety days."

"Well," Billy spoke quietly as if speaking to Yanis. "We didn't make it to the ninety-day point to talk about this goal, did we? I shot for the stars like you said. I know the magic in the Kaula-O is real, I see it in every aspect of my life. But maybe this goal was just a little too large for the time I had to sell. We'll get this one next month."

As soon as Billy's words left his mouth, he smiled at himself. He could picture his old friend, Yanis, standing there, not saying a word. He was being silent just like he did when Billy told him one hundred sales in a month was too large a number. But this time Billy felt he got the last laugh. It appeared Yanis' prediction missed the mark. It reminded him of Alexander's prediction of catching the big headed fish with his reed lure, but Alexander caught his, Billy remembered and smiled.

When they arrived at the farm, it seemed so different with Yanis, Izzy and *Yellow Bird* no longer there. It didn't seem like the same place. When they drove down the driveway, things really looked different. The corn was picked and the stalks were cut. As they neared the house, Goose came running out from under the porch again, barking with excitement. Billy stopped the car to keep from running her over. He opened the door to tell her to move out of the driveway when Goose jumped into the front seat and sat between Billy and Dana. The kids went wild. Goose looked at Billy as if to say. "Where have you been?"

Billy drove to the house and they all got out of the car. That is, all except Goose. She stayed put and refused to get out.

Jack and Lucy were sitting in the swing on the front porch.

"Looks like you got the harvest in," Billy commented, pointing to the cut cornstalks.

"Yes, it was another very good year for the company," he confirmed. "We have been fortunate again. Billy, I appreciate your coming out here on a Saturday like this. But," Jack continued, "there are two things that need your attention.

"The first is Goose. We can't take her on the boat with us and we don't know anyone who would want her. We were kind of hoping you might know someone," he asked suggestively, looking at Billy's kids.

Both kids' eyes lit up. "Oh Dad, please, please, can we take her home? We'll take care of her, we promise. We'll feed her and everything."

Billy looked at Dana. She thought it was a great idea.

"Well, I guess it's unanimous," Billy confirmed,

pointing to Goose still sitting in the front seat of the car. It doesn't look like she wants to get left behind."

"The second piece of business we need to deal with is this. Several months ago, my parents purchased some employee gifts from your company. They submitted a requisition to the board of directors of our corporation for payment. They submitted the figures, but not the complete purchase agreement. With them both passing so closely, the board didn't meet until last week. They have forwarded a check made out to your company for the balance of the order my parents requested. I've been instructed to give it to you along with the names and addresses of our employees. I just want you to know, Billy, I think it is a wonderful gift. I really appreciate you helping my folks in their decision with this. Our employees will surely be appreciative. "

Billy looked at Jack in confusion. "Your parents already paid for those gifts," he said. "They paid me for a gift for every Barton Farm employee. They wrote me a check three months ago for the fourteen employees and one for themselves. I think the board has made a mistake. I think the check should have gone to your parents as repayment."

Now Jack stepped back, somewhat surprised. He knew what his parents intended. They made it very clear to the board. They intended to purchase a gift for each employee in their corporation, meaning all five businesses. That would be a total of five hundred sixty-eight employees. Jack thought for a moment about the situation. Though puzzled, he thought he might know what had happened. Billy had no idea of his parents' other corporations. He thought they only owned Barton Farms. Jack smiled. Boy was Billy going to be surprised.

"Billy," Jack said slowly. "I think you had better sit down. If you think your new sailboat, *Yellow Bird,* was a good surprise, get ready for this one. When my parents made an order to purchase a gift for every employee in their company, they meant the parent corporation that owns all their other companies. My parents own five very successful companies besides the farm.

"They left very clear instructions to our board of directors that all employees were to receive a gift. Billy, that means, given the credit for the fourteen gifts your company has delivered, this is a check for the balance of the order. That would be five hundred sixty-eight more. I have a check for three hundred forty thousand, eight hundred dollars made out to your company. I guess I need a copy of the purchase agreement to submit to the board for their records. It appears my parents never got one."

Now Billy's mind was reeling. He was completely taken off guard. He had no idea Yanis and Izzy intended this. In fact, Billy didn't even know about the other companies. He thought the Bartons were farmers, he didn't know otherwise.

Billy couldn't think straight enough to say anything. He shook Jack's hand and slowly walked to his car. Picking up his briefcase, he pulled out a sales agreement and a pen. It was like he was moving in autopilot because his mind wasn't following his actions completely. He was in shock.

When he finally stumbled back onto the porch, he

noticed Dana's eyes tearing up and her mouth agape. She was trying to act normal, but not doing a very good job of it.

Billy composed himself as best he could and stepped to Jack. "Jack, I need to ask you something." He paused for a moment before continuing. "Are you sure this is what your folks intended? I didn't know anything about the other employees. Before I can take this check and complete this order, I need to be sure. That's all."

"I talked with them personally about it when it first hit my desk months ago, Billy," he responded. "They were very sure about it. And, Billy, now I can truly understand why they both felt the way they did about you. I very much appreciate your friendship and the consideration you showed my folks."

With that, Billy filled out the sales agreement and in the quantity column, he wrote in the number five hundred sixty-eight. It had not only been another very good day, but a very surprising one. Somehow, Billy knew this would be life changing just like Yanis predicted.

They all said their goodbyes and promised to stay in touch. The McCoy family piled into their station wagon, along with Goose, and headed for home. Billy shook his head and laughed at the thought: *Somehow I guess I made my goal of two hundred this month, plus a few.*

As they got into town, they passed the service station where he had gotten fuel earlier. Then it hit him. He remembered the Magic Moment Goal. He had momentarily forgotten about it again.

The instant he remembered, Billy could see the old man standing there looking at him. But this time it was Yanis who had the 'know it all' grin, just like Alexander had when the reed lure had worked.

"You did it again," Billy said silently to himself. To Billy there were no more words necessary. It was as his mentors said, "Experience is the best teacher."

"Dana," he said, his hands shaking as he reached into his pocket for his wallet.

"Do you remember when I told you about the goal process Yanis showed me? Remember the four boxes I filled in with the numbers of each particular goal? I was supposed to put the fourth goal, the Magic Moment Goal, inside my wallet?"

"I remember you telling me about the goals and what you were doing," she responded. "But you never told me what that Magic Moment Goal number was."

"Get ready for your magic moment," he said, handing her the wallet.

Dana opened it slowly. "Inside is a small piece of paper with a box drawn on it," Billy said. "In the box is written the words, Magic Moment Goal. The number I wrote ninety days ago is NINE HUNDRED SALES.

"Dana, Yanis always told me to not be afraid to reach for the stars, so I reached for the stars when I wrote that number down. Up until today, my sales have totaled just at three hundred fifty sales for the last three months. Then, if you add in today's surprise sale of five hundred sixty-eight, the three-month total is NINE HUNDRED EIGHTEEN SALES"

Billy and Dana drove the rest of the way home in silence. Billy's mind was reeling, remembering Yanis' words. "When you realize the Magic Moment Goal is real, your lives will change dramatically."

Their life did change dramatically. Their dream of living in Colorado was assured.

11

REALIZATION

Accept your dream and see it real
In faith you must believe,
Empowered by emotions feel
Your dream has been received.

The following Monday, Billy walked into his office. After asking to see his manager, he stepped into his private office. "Good morning, I have a question for you," Billy said.

"And what's that, Billy?"

"I made a few sales last Saturday, but I haven't been able to turn the sales agreement in until this morning. I was wondering, will these sales count toward last month or this month? Seeing how the last day of the month was Saturday."

"Why does it matter, Billy? You were the top salesperson last month without any additional sales. Plus it was another company record."

"Well, I'm just curious. I'm thinking about the thousand-dollar bonus check from Mr. Harvey," he smiled.

"If you turn it in today, it counts for this month. Besides, your last month production already qualified you for a bonus check," the manager stated.

"I just have a little surprise for you," Billy said, shuffling his feet.

"What could you do that would surprise me any more than you have already, Billy McCoy?" The manager asked. "You have the entire company at your service. My phone never stops ringing with questions from other managers."

"Well, Sir, we have a new daily, weekly and monthly sales record to chase," Billy said, handing the purchase order and check to his manager.

"Five hundred sixty-eight," was all the manager said as his jaw dropped. He looked at the payment check and then at Billy. "The number is too large to comprehend," he furthered. "But I do know one thing," he added with a big smile. "I think you will have sales honors again this month."

The company Billy worked for and many others offered him very lucrative management positions, along with partial ownership. Billy turned them all down. He just wanted to be a salesman. He loved working directly with his customers. He continued to try new sales approaches and techniques. As he did, he set new sales records.

He and Dana raised their kids and sent them off to college. They enjoyed sailing *Yellow Bird* on weekends during the warmer summer months. In the winter, they brought her back to the farm and stored her inside the barn.

It was the spring their daughter finished her first year of college that Dana suggested, "Billy, why don't we take

Yellow Bird to the ocean? Our kids are both on their own. Your business has created a handsome retirement for us. There really is nothing to hold us back. What do you say?"

It took Billy only a few seconds to answer. "I say, yes."

The following month, *Yellow Bird* was hauled by truck across country to Annapolis, Maryland, and launched in the Chesapeake Bay. They spent the summer learning to navigate a much larger body of water than their lake in Colorado.

By early winter, with their confidence high, Billy and Dana sailed *Yellow Bird* out into the Atlantic Ocean toward the island of Bermuda, six hundred miles away.

Their small sailing yacht took them on an adventure of a lifetime. As the months went by, they knew where they wanted to go, but they had many places to see first. From Bermuda they sailed south nine hundred miles to the Virgin Islands, then along the Leeward and Windward Island chain to Granada, Trinidad and finally Venezuela. From Venezuela, they sailed to Bonaire, Curacao, and Aruba.

After sailing away from Aruba and heading northwest, they sailed over nine hundred miles. Eight days later, with the distant island chain in sight, *Yellow Bird* tucked her shoulder plowing forward, trying her best to make the anchorage early enough to have good light for navigation through the reefs.

The wind and waves did not cooperate. Still with twenty-two miles to go to reach their destination, *Yellow Bird* was forced to seek shelter from the massive waves and forty-knot winds. The nearest protected anchorage was a small island five miles ahead. They changed course sailing around the southern shore of the island of Utilla. Working their way through the small reef system on the southern border, they sailed up close to the shore and dropped anchor before nightfall. The island blocked the winds and waves. *Yellow Bird* sat quietly. Having traveled a distance of over four thousand miles since leaving the Chesapeake Bay five months before, it was almost like she knew she was close to her destination.

EPILOGUE

By thought your life you can direct
Create it as you please,
Through knowledge learned you can expect
Prosperity and peace.

"There it is, there it is," Dana screamed as I steered *Yellow Bird* toward the cut. The waves were calmer than yesterday, but still pounding through the break in the reef, creating a washboard of white-water mayhem.

"We have to get the timing right," I warned. Watching the last set of waves march through the cut in the reef, I pushed the tiller hard to port. *Yellow Bird* dipped her shoulder and charged quickly into the entrance of the protected lagoon.

"Ready with the headsail," I screamed so Dana could hear me over the roar of the waves. "Okay, release it now."

Yellow Bird slid into and through the cut with precision. At the last moment, I yanked the tiller, guiding her to starboard as Dana dropped the big headsail. *Yellow Bird* skated safely behind the protection of the barrier reef. The following set of waves raised high above the small sailing vessel, but crashed harmlessly behind her.

We slowly sailed to the opposite side of the protected lagoon. Turning back into the wind briefly, *Yellow Bird* slowed to a stop, allowing Dana to drop anchor.

I back winded the mainsail, pulling the chain rode tight which dug the anchor deep into the sand.

Then I released the tiller and stepped up on the coach roof. Taking Dana in my arms, I held her close. "We made it, my love," I said. "Roatan at last. Look out across this lagoon, Dana. This is where it all started, our dream of sailing. It doesn't seem so long ago that we watched Jack and Lucy sail into this lagoon and drop anchor."

"Not long at all," she said. "I remember how shocked we both were when Jack said his career was in 'sales.' Billy, I sure am glad you took that job offer fourteen years ago."

"I am too," I replied. "I am too."

We took a few moments to tidy up things on deck and let *Yellow Bird* sit quietly. Putting towels into Alexander's crocodile bag, Dana and I slid into the water off the stern of our small sailing yacht and swam to shore.

Once we could stand, I took Dana's hand and we turned briefly to look at our beautiful friend sitting quietly in the crystal-clear Caribbean water. Hand in hand, we continued to the small café on the beach and sat at the exact table we had lunch at fourteen years earlier.

While waiting for our lunch, I reached into the crocodile backpack and pulled out the envelope Izzy had left me years before. I smile remembering the day I first read it right after her passing.

"Izzy said I would know when the time is right," I

said to Dana.

Dana smiled remembering Izzy's words also.

I opened the envelope and read.

You were such a good student. The time to share this precious gift with the world is at hand. It has been taught for generations, but now more than ever people are searching for answers. They are insisting on change through knowledge. Teach them to focus on great dreams and possibilities, not the fears they are bombarded with daily. As you know Billy, things are not always as they might seem. Great power is found in the unseen, FAITH AND EXPECTANCY.

STEP ONE:

Plant the dream seed.

Plant the seed of your dream in the garden of your mind by imagining precisely in every detail, a picture of exactly what you desire. Include yourself happily enjoying its completion, right now in this very moment. And, while the picture is clearly seen recognize the surge of emotional joy and satisfaction you feel. As soon as that feeling is felt and acknowledged, move your thought elsewhere. Don't linger allowing time for negative defeating thoughts to invade your mind. I have found the best time to do this imagination process is the first thing in the morning and last thing before you sleep at night.

STEP TWO:

Tend to your garden in two ways. This step is an ongoing process.

First, you must fertilize the garden soil continually by consciously recognizing every small change or achievement that occurs in your life. As you recognize these, no matter how small, feel great gratitude and joy releasing more and more powerful emotion. This continually reinforces your dream and your expectancy. This opens and builds a wide pathway for dream fulfillment.

Second, you must constantly de-weed your garden. To do this you must police your thoughts. When thoughts of doubt or fear and anxiety, etc. pop into your mind (I call these thoughts weeds) simply say 'STOP.' But do not embellish further. Just change your thoughts to another subject, preferably something positive. If you dwell on a long, lengthy cancellation process of these thoughts, your focus stays on the negative and just further energizes it. The quicker you release the weed seed thought, the better.

STEP THREE:

Pick the fruit from your garden. In other words accept the fulfillment of your desired dream.

Accepting the results of your dream into your life often happens automatically as you complete step two. Because, as you continually recognize the small changes and achievements occurring you're constantly reinforcing your expectancy of accomplishment. The level of this expectancy determines fulfillment. Through your faith in the process, your dreams are fulfilled. With absolute expectancy, acceptance is complete and the physical manifestation of your dream is realized.

> *Yanis and I put these teaching steps together to help you remember Alexander's lessons. Go forth and share the teachings with all who seek.*
> *Billy, remember, we love you, Yanis and Izzy*

Dana and I sat quietly, reflecting on the moment.

"Billy," Dana said. "When we return home, what should we do now that you have retired from your sales career?"

I looked toward my wife. "The way I see it, Dana, the most important part of our sales career is just now beginning," I said. "We have a new product to share, 'THE MAGIC IN DREAMING.' I think it's time we give back to a world that has provided so much for us. Are you onboard?"

She looked at me and smiled. I knew her answer.